A. D

150

D1311694

SANTA FE TRAIL

Santa Fe Trail

Walker A. Tompkins

THORNDIKE
C H I V E R S

This Large Print edition is published by Thorndike Press, Waterville, Maine, USA and by BBC Audiobooks Ltd, Bath, England.

Thorndike Press, a part of Gale, Cengage Learning.

The text of this Large Print edition is unabridged.
Other aspects of the book may vary from the original edition.
Set in 16 pt. Plantin.
Printed on permanent paper.

LIBRARY OF CONGRESS CATALOGING-IN-PUBLICATION DATA

Tompkins, Walker A.
   Santa Fe trail / by Walker A. Tompkins.
     p. cm. — (Thorndike Press large print western)
   ISBN-13: 978-1-4104-0697-2 (alk. paper)
   ISBN-10: 1-4104-0697-0 (alk. paper)
   1. Large type books. I. Title.
PS3539.O3897S26 2008
813'.52—dc22   2008009197

BRITISH LIBRARY CATALOGUING-IN-PUBLICATION DATA AVAILABLE

Published in 2008 in the U.S. by arrangement with Golden West Literary Agency.
Published in 2008 in the U.K. by arrangement with Golden West Literary Agency.

U.K. Hardcover: 978 1 408 41181 0 (Chivers Large Print)
U.K. Softcover: 978 1 408 41182 7 (Camden Large Print)

Printed in the United States of America
1 2 3 4 5 6 7 12 11 10 09 08

SANTA FE TRAIL

CHAPTER I

RIVER TOWN

It had been raining, and the Missouri that night had a furious, swollen aspect as it boomed past Westport Landing, where the river steamboats tied up.

Westport citizens had built some distance back from the dangerous bank, determined not to suffer the same fate as Franklin, which for a time had served in outfitting caravans for the Santa Fe run. Franklin had been a thriving prairie port but one day had slid under the mocking waters. And Independence, the next stop, had lost its entire landing.

Dark clouds swept in from the southeast, low over the town. Oil lamps glowed as yellow egg yolks, but beyond their range the shadows were inky. The spring was a cool one in the "Suffering Sixties," when the Civil War was not long past and hatred was still inflaming the hearts of brothers. There was talk of Grant for President, while thousands of uprooted Americans, ruined by the terrible conflict, moved West, pushing the frontier ever nearer the Pacific settlements.

There was a raucous fight going on in Pierre's, a large tavern on Westport's main street, which was inches deep in gluey mud churned by the ironclad wheels of heavy wagons. Music came from several spots, and the hoarse shouts of men mingled with the shriller cries of women in the general hubbub.

Westport was a jumping-off place and to it swarmed the bizarre people of the mighty frontier, hunting profit and amusement. Saloonmen and gamblers, soldiers, traders and trappers, miners, wagon drivers and mule-skinners, river boat men, merchants and adventurers of all types were here. The wildest revelry made the welkin ring and each egotistical soul carried a gun and knife, for pride was fierce and easily stirred.

Men in from long weeks of the dangerous eight-hundred-mile run from Santa Fe spent their wages or profits in a night. Raw and noisy, daring fate and playing for keeps in the game of life, they sought high stakes or death.

The fight in the front bar of Pierre's was proceeding as such affairs usually did.

Those who did not wish to join in had ducked behind the bar or tables. Several river men, armed with Navy pistols, had quarreled with some cowboys from a Kansas ranch. Chairs had been crashed and bottles thrown, and now guns were roaring. A man went down, clutching his thigh. Smoke drifted to the gilt lamps, hanging from the rafters by chains.

In a back room, a private parlor of the establishment, were three men. They paid not the slightest attention to the brawl up the long corridor. Two sat at a table, on which were bottles and the remains of a meal. They had frozen in a tense attitude.

"I reckon we talked too loud, Sam," growled the heavy voice of one bearded fellow.

"We shore did, Jack," agreed the other man at the table. "Whiskey loosens the tongue!"

"Fork it over," ordered the cold voice of the third man, who was standing.

He was tall and lean, and wore dark clothes and a black hat. His nose was as bridgeless as a wedge of pale cheese, and over his flecked grayish eyes his long lashes lowered as he watched his prey.

A white scar ran from the corner of his

left eye past the cheek bone, puckering the flesh so that the lid twitched. He had thin black hair and a strong jaw.

He had shut the door behind him as he had slipped in. Jack and Sam had been poring over a paper before them, chortling together. For a moment they had thought it was only the waiter who had entered with another bottle. When they raised their eyes it had been too late, for they had been staring into the muzzle of a big Colt.

"Yuh want our money?" said Sam. "We'll give it to yuh."

"Keep yore paws in sight!" snapped the lean man, ever wary, allowing his victims no chance to go for a gun. "Push over that map."

Rage flushed Jack's bearded cheeks and he bit at his lip. The shock had sobered him.

"Wait a jiffy, Johnny Holdup. I lost my kid brother out there in the mountains. The Comanches got his hair. Me and Sam sweated, starved, and froze for over a year for this and we ain't passin' it to the first dirty rascal who happens along!"

"Look out!" screamed Sam. "He's goin' to shoot!"

He kicked back his chair in a convulsive movement as he thrust a hand inside his shirt to pull his pistol.

But Jack was done for. The blackhaired man had already fired and the heavy slug had drilled through the brain. Jack slumped and the killer whirled on Sam, who had his gun out but not aimed. A second bullet hit Sam, whirled him around, and he fell to the rough board floor, a screech of agony on his lips, his weapon going off, but ineffectually, as his fingers spasmodically clutched the trigger.

The gray eyes blazed, the left one violently twitching, as the lean man grasped the smudged paper and pushed it into his pocket. In the main bar at Pierre's men were shouting and guns blasting away so that the quick fracas in the parlor at the rear had gone unheard by those in front.

Yet chance, which had brought this killer to the spot where the dead Jack and dying Sam had been celebrating their good fortune, again intervened. The scrap in the saloon had assumed the proportions of a battle as more and more men joined in. City marshals, charged with keeping a semblance of peace in Westport, were converging on the spot.

One young lawman had run down a side way to come through the back entry, and as the lean man opened the door, the marshal, his silver badge catching the lamplight, looked in and saw Jack dead in his chair. Sam was moaning and writhing on the other side of the table.

"What's goin' on here!" cried the marshal, pulling up short.

The robber jumped back, slammed the door and bolted it. He rushed to the open window and climbed through, making for the street where he had left his saddled horse.

There were more law officers charging into Pierre's to check the spreading riot, but they paid no attention to the lone figure ducking under the rail to reach his tall bay. He mounted, aware of the crackling chart in his pocket and pleased with his luck. The fact that he had killed two people to get it did not affect him.

As he pulled a rein to swing into the muddy road a bullet whirled by his head. He turned to see who had tried for him. It was the young marshal, who had run through the saloon to the porch.

"Too smart for yore own good," muttered the fugitive, throwing up his revolver.

He fired but missed, for the lawman had vaulted the railing and was shielded by standing horses. The fugitive set spurs to his mount. The bay was fast but it took a few moments to pick up speed, and the rider was outlined in lights which blazed in the town. The marshal took the center of the road and sent slugs after the outlaw.

The bay gave a great leap and the rider felt tearing, shattering metal pierce his thigh. For a moment the world blacked out but he managed to pull himself together and swore in rage.

He was an excellent marksman and as the mist cleared could see the young marshal with spread feet, Colt up for another attempt. The bandit emptied his revolver at his pursuer and brutal satisfaction flushed him as the lawman staggered and clawed at his side.

The bay was hurt but could still run. The animal had a brave heart and no knowledge of good and evil, obeying only the dictates of his rider. The cruel spurs bit deep and sent him galloping through the night. Another Westport marshal, hurrying to help his comrade, glimpsed the fleeing killer and seized the reins of a nearby horse to pursue.

There was no time for anything but frantic escape. Here the Missouri made its great bend toward the Mississippi. Westport was south of the muddy river. West lay Kansas prairies and southwest fabulous Santa Fe. The bay gelding drove on. Soon he was out of the roaring settlement, his hoofs kicking up globules of mud from the wet plain.

CHAPTER II

CARAVAN

Steadily, "Steelhide" Andrew Cass drew a bead with his Sharps rifle on the huge buffalo bull. His saddled horse stood a quarter of a mile behind him, for he had stolen up afoot to make his shot. The lead balls for the Sharps weighed eight to the pound and as the bullet drove home the animal shuddered, his front knees soon collapsed, and he quietly rolled over on the ground.

Cass stood up and looked toward the friend who had accompanied him, a young Mexican named Celestino Mireles, and his fellow hunter from the long wagon train en route to Santa Fe. The Mexican waved to him. He had already made his kill. They would skin the animals, cut off the best meat, and have a light wagon run out to pick it up. It was serious business, this hunting, and not sport, for there were many hungry mouths to feed in the wagon train, and fresh meat prevented scurvy and gave men the strength needed for the trials of the wilderness.

Andrew Cass was a product of this Frontier. From pioneer forebears he had inherited a big frame, which was muscled with hardened sinews developed by constant riding and outdoor work. Dark hair curled around his generous ears. He had been reared in danger. Indians had slain his parents, and at the age of twelve he had struck out for himself. He had been a hunter, scout, and guide, and had prospected in the Rockies with remnants of the old Mountain Men. He had learned from them to despise cities and the softnesses they engendered in mankind. As the saying had it, Cass was a man to ride the river with — strong, never complaining, ready to sacrifice his life for a friend.

His nickname had been derived from an experience several years before when a roving band of Comanches had captured him and two comrades. Andrew Cass had endured without a single outcry the prickings with heated knife points and long pins which the savages had decided upon as sport of the day. The prisoners would have died had not a party of hunters sighted the smoke and crept up on the torturers. Cass and another man had been snatched away before the Indians could despatch them. The story of his ability to withstand pain had spread and he had been called "Steelhide" ever since.

Celestino Mireles was bony and tall in his pliant Mexican velvet, a steeple sombrero strapped to his black-haired head. He had a patrician cast of feature, a hawk nose, high cheekbones and black eyes in which shone pride. Steelhide was aware that the young Mexican was about the shrewdest horse trader on the Frontier, and that was saying a great deal since many men out there knew everything about the animals and considered it clever to outdo one another in a swap. Mireles was a protégé and friend of the Rio Kid, captain of the wagon train which Cass was accompanying to Santa Fe as hunter and aide.

Right now the two men were on the Kansas Plains, lush prairie close to the Arkansas River along which the Santa Fe Trail ran for some distance.

With the buffalo down, Cass prudently went back and picked up his tawny mustang, so as to have his horse close at hand. Mireles, trained in the same school, already had mounted his beautiful pinto and was approaching the kill. They would help one another and so get through sooner.

Cass returned, dropped his reins, and squatted by the dying bull's heavy throat. A shrill cry from the Mexican sent Steelhide to his feet and, after a quick look, he leaped to his saddle and rode to join Mireles who was pelting south toward the Trail. He soon came up beside Mireles.

"Comanches!" Mireles cried.

Steelhide nodded. The Indians had emerged from one of the numerous splits in the apparently endless, rolling land ocean. They used these for cover, in place of broken terrain and timber available in other sections of the great range.

No doubt the cracking Sharps had been heard by the redmen. Cass and Mireles watched ahead and on both sides.

"There's the other bunch," grunted Steelhide.

They had expected the Comanches would have started a second line of painted warriors to cut them off.

Their horses were better than the chunky plains mustangs and the two white hunters swerved southwest. A couple of leading chiefs sent long carbine shots at them but they whirled by the danger point, avoiding prairie-dog burrows, since a fallen mount meant death.

"Look, Steelhide!" called Mireles, pointing north after they had been forced off course for over a mile. "Zey have someone!"

They could now see past low, grassy mounds which had previously cut off vision in that direction. More mounted Indians were riding a circle out from a black streak they knew was a ravine, while a dead horse lay on the plain.

As they watched, a puff of smoke showed that whoever was holed up in the split was still defending himself.

The two hunters knew it was sure death to stop, though, that any attempt on their part to aid the embattled man would be futile. They were forced to ride on at top speed. Besides, the wagon train people must be warned that Indians were near.

When they had outflanked the Comanches they hurried to reach the wagon train. The sun was high and hot when they sighted the vehicles creeping through waist-high prairie grass. The wagons were traveling in four lines abreast, this being considered safest in the Indian country, since they could be quickly formed into a hollow square for defense.

When laden, a big Conestoga weighed from three thousand to seven thousand pounds and required six yoke of oxen to draw it properly. The hooped ash frames were covered with Osnaburg sheeting, the high wheels shod with iron rims.

Drivers walked beside their teams, carrying whips with thick stocks, and lashes sixteen feet long. Emigrants who were walking the eight hundred miles of the Trail moved within the protection of the wagons, while in the rear, on both sides and in the van were horsemen, armed and alert.

Lighter outfits also had joined this large party. A Rockaway carriage drawn by a pair of fine white horses reflected the sunshine from polished leather. Often people made the trip for the sake of health, traveling in what was considered style, with a tent, a carpet, stools, a Dutch oven and other such luxuries.

Yet these did little to ease the rigors of the trail.

Steelhide Cass and Mireles pulled up their lathered horses, to salute the captain in charge of the wagon train.

"We shot two buffalo, Rio Kid," Cass reported, "but a bunch of Comanches run us off. They got someone holed up in a ravine."

"*Si*, General." Mireles nodded, as he made his affirmation to the man who was closest to him of any in the world, and whom he had long ago named "General," and never called by another name. "Ees death for heem out zere."

To this Mexican, Bob Pryor, his partner and benefactor, the man known on the Frontier as the Rio Kid, was the most important person in the world. Steelhide Cass came close to owning to a somewhat like feeling toward the Rio Kid who, though now leading a wagon train, had been Captain Robert Pryor of the United States Army not long before. As a soldier, he had made a great name for himself in battle for the Union. For although he was a Texan, he had fought for the North, following the dictates of his conscience for a union undivided.

He was a debonair, handsome young man, a trained and hardened athlete with crisp chestnut hair, a face bronzed by sun and wind, and eyes a steady blue. His wide shoulders tapered to a narrow waist, and he was the ideal height and weight for a cavalryman, such as he had been. From military life he had brought habits of neatness, as well as dress and equipment. He wore a blue shirt, a felt Stetson, and whipcord trousers tucked into polished boots. Crossed cartridge belts supported the black holsters of his pistols.

When the war was over and Bob Pryor had headed home, it was in the eager hope of seeing his parents, and taking up life on the ranch where he had left off. But he never saw the parents again. Bandits had raided his home ranch and killed both father and mother.

With nothing left of his home, he had taken up a roving life, with the avowed intention of avenging just such wrongs as he had suffered, wherever he might run across them. It was not long before his name was becoming known throughout the West — not as Captain Bob Pryor, but as the Rio Kid, on whom all oppressed could count for aid when the going was rough.

It was soon after he began his travels that, on a sudden trip across the Border into Mexico, he met Celestino Mireles. He arrived at the *haciendo* which the youth had called home, just in time to discover that bandits also had killed Celestino's father and mother, and fired the home. Rescuing Celestino himself, after a running battle, he had made a lifelong friend. From that moment on, Celestino Mireles had dedicated his life to the Rio Kid, had followed him wherever he had gone.

Now Celestino was his constant trail companion and devoted friend, and Steelhide Cass was swiftly coming into camp as one of Bob Pryor's staunch admirers. Steelhide, however, was not alone in holding the Rio Kid in the highest respect. Pryor was a natural leader who assumed responsibilities as a matter of course, always seeing to the needs of others — which was seen and appreciated. Intrepid and cool, able to make vital decisions on the instant when so required, the Rio Kid was the sort of man it took to lead men of Steelhide's caliber.

As the Rio Kid spoke now with Cass and Mireles, the mousecolored dun he rode danced about, and tried to bite a chunk of hide from Cass' mustang.

"Steady, Saber!" soothed Pryor, and touched Saber's neck.

The Rio Kid was much attached to that horse, for Saber had carried him through the war, a first-class battle steed, for the dun loved the sound of bugles and a good scrap. He was not good-tempered, though, and when he could he would mix it with other animals. But always, as now, he was obedient to his rider's wishes. He was distinguished by a black stripe down his back, for he had come from the strain which had been called, "the breed that never dies."

Not prepossessing, the horse made up for that in speed. So far, the Rio Kid had never come upon another mount which could outrun Saber.

Right now, though, the Rio Kid was not thinking of his fiery mount. He had Comanches on his mind.

"How many yuh figger are around?" he inquired of Cass.

"We spotted sixty to seventy," replied Steelhide.

The Rio Kid's eyes were troubled as they swept his charges, the good folks of the train traveling to Santa Fe. Steelhide could sense something of what Pryor felt. The captain was responsible for the lives and property of these two hundred men, women and children. An error in judgment might spell death for one or for all of them, and so his responsibility was great.

The Rio Kid blew a silver whistle and his gauntleted hand swung over his head. The drivers knew what that signal meant and quickly obeyed. Long bull lashes crackled in the warm air and hoarse voices swore at oxen and mules. The two outer files of wagons moved on, allowing the inner ones to veer right and left and close the rear gap. Wheels together, and halted, the caravan was prepared and ready for defense, with smaller vehicles and stock inside the hollow square.

"There may be more of them redskins around," said the Rio Kid. "They hang around on the Trail and raid small parties. It's a regular thing. Travelers attract the cusses the way a broken molasses jug does flies."

No one was more well aware than he of the risks taken in travel in this country, where there was no choice save that by slow wagon train or on horseback, or afoot as men had moved for ages, and always exposed to nature's vagaries. Windstorms, cloudbursts, drought, heat and at times hunger overtook them. Another risk to be faced were red raiders who, aware of the riches passing by, made a practise of attacking trains. Comanches, Apaches, Kiowas and other warlike tribes lurked always near. There was menace in the air, forever looming over trekkers on the trail.

Further east in Kansas, Colonel Cyrus K. Holliday had begun laying the rails for his road from Topeka to the westward, the line which was to become famous, later, as the Atchison, Topeka and Santa Fe. But as yet it had not pierced far into the Southwest, and until such a time as it did, travelers must move in the manner of their forebears.

As the big wagons came to a halt about the square they had formed, the Rio Kid could see that men were already checking rifles and pistols. He looked around, picking men in his mind to accompany him on a mission of rescue of a lone man facing savage vengeance.

"Steelhide," the Rio Kid commanded abruptly, "take charge while I am gone."

Cass would have enjoyed the brush with the savages but orders were orders, and he pushed his mount around to the north side of the square. A girl called to him from a Rockaway carriage in which she sat with a large, bearded man of about fifty.

"What is it, Andrew?"

"Nothin' much, Miss Sari." Steelhide did not wish to alarm her. "A few motheaten Injuns, that's all."

Steelhide kept his gaze turned on her, something he had never been able to resist doing, ever since Sari and her father, Galusha Shannon, had joined the train. It was pleasant to look at her, yet disturbing to a man like him, a homeless wanderer on the wild face of the earth. For he could only think of Sari settled in a pretty cabin on a clear river, with furniture and curtains and a garden.

Her youthful beauty overwhelmed Cass,

as it always did, and she was indeed a picture. A small bonnet sat pertly on her wavy auburn hair, and her eyes smiled at him. Her lips were invitingly crimson, her cheeks were touched with freckles. She had a quick way of tossing her head to laugh which, Cass thought, was captivating. The wide-skirted dress she wore, with the waist small and tight, completed the picture.

Cass towered over her as they stood talking together, and her dainty femininity made him feel hulking. Yet he well knew that if she so desired she could lead him around as easily as she might lead around an ox with a ring in its nose.

Her father, Galusha Shannon, who sat in the Rockaway with her, was a heavy man. Gray touched his temples and lines etched his good-natured face.

He was going to New Mexico because, in spite of his bulk, his health had failed and he hoped to find a cure in the dry climate.

Shannon was well-off, compared to most of those in the train. He had been in the leather business in St. Louis but had sold out before leaving for Santa Fe. He was a widower and Sari was his only child. And others than Cass admired the girl's capability in caring for her father.

Everybody liked the Shannons who from the start had done all they could to enter wholeheartedly into the wagon train life. Sari helped with the younger children, assisting busy wives along the road. Her brightness was cheering. Galusha was a kind man, with a great fund of sympathy, the type of solid citizen whose opinion is valued by his fellows.

Steelhide had set those two aside from the rest, as soon as he had met them, and he had often wondered at the variety of humanity to be found in the party. Carpenters, miners, farmers, stockraisers, and men from other trades were represented. There were veterans of the War, many hunting a fresh start in life.

The eldest man making the journey was over sixty, the youngest traveler a babe in arms.

Some took everything that came along with stoical fortitude, while others fussed at small obstacles. There were braggarts and silent ones. But in each and all was a spirit of adventure, or the long trip would never have been started.

There was not an entire lack of amusement as the train rumbled along. Some had brought along their violins — or fiddles, as they called them — and the strings squeaked away in the wilderness when the train paused for the night. Cards and dice were fascinating to the men.

The main caravan had made up in Westport, but other wagons and riders had joined its protection since then. Single individuals and parties had been strangers to one another at the start, but the Rio Kid's personality and ability had drawn them together and held them in a compact unit.

Now the wagon train folk were friends, with a single purpose, and welded together by the perils of the Trail.

CHAPTER III

GUNS ON THE PRAIRIE

The Rio Kid swiftly moved toward the spot on the prairie where Cass had reported the trouble. Common humanity ordered that a victim, probably a white man, be rescued if possible from torture and death at the hands of Indians.

Celestino Mireles rode at Pryor's left. At the wagon train captain's right hand was a tall, muscular horseman with deep-set eyes, a short black mustache, a wide brow, and a face tapering grimly to a sharp chin. He wore buckskins and a wide Stetson, and there was stern power in his aspect.

The man, Major Frank North, was already a hero of the Frontier, and close friend of the Rio Kid. Known on the plains as the white chief of the Pawnees, he spoke their tongue fluently and commanded a large band of their warriors. North's bravery was becoming legend.

But now Major North had been ill, and

was making the run to Santa Fe for the sake of his health. Even so, the Rio Kid knew that Frank North sick was a better man than most fighters in the pink of condition. His spirit was unconquerable, though the jogging of his mustang brought dry coughs from his lean throat.

With his two aides and a score of other armed white men at his back, the Rio Kid was sure he could handle a large number of savages, who did not fancy knock-down-drag-out slugging fests against determined opposition. Indications that they were near the enemy came when a bullet hummed in the hot air, but flew wide.

Then they sighted Comanches over the crest of a ravine ahead. Indians pelted out and came at the white men in savage array, whooping and shooting, with thrilling exhibits of most expert horsemanship. But no one had time to notice that as the Rio Kid and Major North opened with carbines and kept on rushing.

"Tryin' us out!" called Pryor, and North nodded.

As the wild riders of the plains saw they could not stampede the party, they swerved and rode off at full speed. Mireles indicated the ravine with the dead horse lying out from it. Having driven off the Indians with a display of arms, the Rio Kid moved in.

Steelhide Cass and the Mexican had been correct. There had been a white man at the mercy of the Comanches. He was now lying on the slanting bank in the cut. Beside him was a short-barreled rifle, and in one hand was a six-shooter.

The Rio Kid and Major North hurried to his side. Flecked grayish eyes filled with agony sought their faces. The man had a bridgeless nose and a white scar from his left eye corner, puckering his cheek. The dark clothes on his long, lean body were ripped and plastered with dust and blood, and his hat was missing. Thin black hair was matted on his head. He seemed utterly exhausted.

"All right, mister," the Rio Kid said kindly, squatting beside him. "Where yuh hit? Who are yuh?"

"My leg! The Indians — shot my hoss and me. I managed to crawl in here. My name's Webb Daggett."

North and the Rio Kid examined the thigh wound. It was crusted over and filled with dirt and shreds of cloth.

"When were yuh shot?" inquired Pryor. "That looks like it was a couple of days old."

Daggett nodded. "They shot me and ran me for miles. Touch and go." He closed his eyes, and they saw the fever in his cheeks.

The bone did not seem to be cracked but the infected wound needed cleaning and bandaging. Strong hands lifted Daggett and, placed before the Rio Kid on Saber, the injured man was carried back to the train.

"We'll camp here for the night," ordered the Rio Kid, as they approached the wagons.

Webb Daggett was laid out under a tent's protection. Sari Shannon came with other women to help, and the Rio Kid's eyes were drawn to her. Like Steelhide Cass, Pryor had fallen under her spell, but as always, he held himself in hand.

They were close to the Arkansas River which here was three-fourths of a mile wide and three to four feet in depth. The water was chalky white, but fine for drinking.

Buffalo chips provided fuel and big iron kettles, blackened by previous fires, were set to boil. With hot water and clean clothes, Webb Daggett's wound was cleansed and then covered with a fresh bandage. A drink and some warm broth did wonders for him and soon he was sleeping in the protection of the train, still drawn up in a hollow square.

Steelhide Cass and Celestino had from the start of the journey alternated as commander of the guard. Tonight was Steelhide's turn, and he organized the sentries before dark. Every man in the party, unless sick, must stand a tour of duty for the common good.

Dark fell over the wilderness. Little fires broke the vast night where the wagon train camped. Civilization seemed far removed, but there were human beings here, with all the cares and tribulations, the hopes and fears of mankind. Families grouped together with friends. The oxen and other stock were being grazed and watched by delegated riders.

After his meal the Rio Kid fixed a smoke and walked through the encampment to make sure all was well. Someone was playing "Buffalo Gals," on a fiddle, and the sprightly tune was cheering.

Pryor rounded a big Conestoga and came upon a group of men playing poker by the light of a fire. Money showed on the spread horse blanket used as a table and they were intent on their game. A smooth, dapper man with a crisp mustache and sharp, acquisitive features had the largest pile of cash before him.

"Don't be a hog, Fullhouse," drawled the Rio Kid.

"Fullhouse" Watts looked up quickly.

Pryor grinned, because gambling was common and hardly to be frowned upon. On the other hand Fullhouse had been shirking his share of the work along the Trail. His hands were carefully kept, his clothing clean. He was undoubtedly a professional gambler and probably a cheat, thought the Rio Kid. The game he ran had been going on every night except when it rained, and Watts was taking more and more from young fellows in the party.

A squat, powerfully made fellow stared challengingly at the captain. He had a cud of tobacco in one leathery cheek. He was dirty, bearded, with small pale-blue eyes and a hide as tough as that of a rhinoceros. The point of his chin curved up and his nose came down to meet it so that a walnut might have been held there — the reason for his nickname, "Nutcracker." And Nutcracker Lynch was an ox driver, profane, brutal, another type of Frontier product from many others in the party.

Pryor moved on, unworried. He was master of such men and knew he could best them if they failed to obey his orders. There were others in the caravan of their caliber, also. But the Rio Kid was aware of that, and kept a hand on the party's pulse, holding command.

As he moved on he saw Sari Shannon sitting beside her father in the folding chairs they carried in the back of their wagon. She smiled up at the captain and again he felt a thrill of admiration for her. The firelight shone on her lustrous hair, reflecting reddish glints.

"I looked in at Mr. Daggett," reported Sari. "He's resting well."

"Glad to hear it, Sari. How are yuh, Mr. Shannon?"

"Fine, fine," said Shannon.

Pryor strolled on. Steelhide Cass saluted him, alert, and checking the sentinels. Children were being put to bed in the wagons or tents, while husbands and wives relaxed for a time before turning in.

"And twenty of 'em come at me, knives flashin'!" a man's loud voice boasted. "I was alone but I began firin' my Colt and they bit the dust!"

The Rio Kid smiled. Tall yarns were the order of the day and in telling them men let off steam while amusing their listeners.

He looked in at the sleeping figure of Webb Daggett. They had saved Daggett from certain death. The Rio Kid knew nothing of the man except that he had needed help, which had been given freely and in a kindly, neighborly manner. That gave the

Rio Kid satisfaction enough as he walked to the spot where he had left his blankets and turned in to sleep. . . .

The sun of the new morning had not yet gained enough strength to dispel the low, clinging prairie mists when breakfast was over and the wagon train ready to move on. The Rio Kid checked on his charges.

"Catch up!" he shouted.

These were magic words. The camp was transformed into a scene of confusion as belongings were tossed into wagons and each person hurried to his post.

"Catch up! Catch up!" The captain's order was relayed through.

Teamsters vied with one another in getting ready. It was a matter of pride for a man to signal he was the first to have his animals hitched, and his rig ready for the day's run. Yokes rattled, chains jingled, and cursing wagoners plied their whips as they drove the beasts of burden into position.

On the dun, the Rio Kid finished his smoke and sat waiting.

"All's set!" The cry first came from an ox driver up front.

"All's set! — All's set!" one after another reported.

Steelhide Cass, Celestino Mireles and

Major North were mounted and near Pryor. Down the way an unruly ox made trouble, breaking from formation. Its driver was Nutcracker Lynch and his profane abuse heated the air. Lynch began beating the animal with a length of heavy chain, laying it on as if thoroughly possessed by his own evil mood.

"Steelhide, run down and tell Nutcracker to quit that and catch up," commanded the Rio Kid.

Cass shoved his tawny mustang to the point, leaning from saddle to speak to Lynch. His message delivered, he pulled his rein to return to the captain, and at that moment Lynch transferred his rage from the dumb beast to the man. It was plain that Nutcracker had been drinking heavily, for his eyes were bloodshot, his appearance disheveled.

Steelhide had spoken civilly, but everybody knew that Lynch had been chided, and this inflamed the man's ego, for he prided himself on his physical strength and toughness, which he believed should make him immune from censure. He swore at Cass, drawing back his huge, hairy hand which was gripping the chain.

The teamster's abuse rose. "Think yuh're a man, yuh young jack? I could bust every bone in yore consarned body! Get out of here. I savvy my business, yuh two-bit bull-sticker! Go yearn over that purty little she-calf yuh been makin' eyes at."

Steelhide was quick, and from the corner of his eye had seen Lynch's threatening gesture. He whirled his mustang, knowing that all eyes were on them as Nutcracker hurled the chain. One end hit Cass in the side of the head, the other stung his horse. The mustang bucked violently, almost unseating Steelhide. But in a moment Cass had control, and jumped from saddle.

"Wait here, boys," said the Rio Kid as North and Mireles started to trail him toward the imminent fight.

Steelhide Cass should have his chance!

Chapter IV

DISSENSION

A pistol was thrust in Lynch's wide belt, and a knife was sheathed at his back ribs. A welt stood out on Steelhide's bronzed cheek where the chain had stung him. Cass advanced and Nutcracker dropped his hand to his revolver.

But Steelhide was upon him before he could draw, and a jolting punch caught the teamster in the face, throwing him off his feet.

That one punch was enough. The Rio Kid pushed between them then.

"Hold it!" he snapped.

Cass obediently stood aside. Pryor narrowly watched the half-stunned Lynch, who sat on the ground rubbing his mouth and nose. But much of his belligerence was gone, for such men as the wagoner understood the brute force of fist or weapon.

"Get up," growled the Rio Kid, flushed with anger.

"Tell that young mule to stay away from me!" flared Lynch. "I'll blow his brains out if he lays hands on me again."

Pryor's gaze fixed him. "I sent him to tell yuh to stop beatin' the ox. It was all yore fault. If yuh ever draw a gun on anybody in this train, yuh answer to me, savvy?"

The punch, the presence of the Rio Kid, had sobered Lynch although he still smoldered, and would never forgive the blow. He dropped his gaze and, pushing himself to his feet, sullenly went about catching up his six yoke of oxen. He was handling a large Conestoga for Silas Gregg, a merchant in the party who was emigrating to the Southwest with a store of household wares.

With the conflict nipped in the bud, the last team was prepared.

"Stretch out!" the Rio Kid shouted. Whips cracked and drivers cried, "Hep, hep, hep!" as they turned their teams.

"Fall in!"

Iron-shod wheels creaked as the wagons rumbled into the formation for the march, four lines abreast.

It was a thrilling sight to see the great caravan ready for the day's run.

"March!" bawled the Rio Kid, and his sweeping gesture started them toward the Southwest.

Steelhide Cass was a good-natured sort and he kept away from Nutcracker Lynch, not wishing to prod the wagoner.

Here the valley of the Arkansas presented a monotonous view. Only stunted sunflowers and willows, cottonwoods, and here and there a clay or sandstone bluff broke the immense, rolling expanse. The prairie offered man beauty and terror, comfort or intense pain, according to its dictates.

They had come at a good pace from the Missouri, two weeks having elapsed since they had left Westport. Fording treacherous streams with the heavy wagons, storms and broken equipment were bound to slow any such train. A good average rate for a day was twelve miles, but westward where the Rockies rose, they knew the piled rocks would almost stop the Conestogas, which would have to be pulled across by main force.

At noon, when they stopped to rest and eat, the Rio Kid paused by the wagon in which the victim of the Indians was riding and found Webb Daggett fully awake and much stronger. Generous souls had provided clean clothing for Daggett and he had eaten and washed up.

"I'm mighty obliged, Cap'n," said Daggett.

"Forget it. We'll take yuh to Santa Fe, and before that yore wound will be healed. Looks better today."

The Rio Kid studied the man he had rescued. Daggett's left eye, above the bridge-less nose, twitched as he returned Pryor's estimating stare. He gave the impression of strength held in, but which would be ready when needed. The bulldog jaw indicated an unyielding toughness.

The Rio Kid had learned in the Army and on the Frontier not to form snap judgments. Daggett, hurt and alone, could be dissembling, but if he had secrets to hide the Rio Kid knew that there were many such in the wilderness, running from the law, from others, from themselves. As long as the wagon train guest behaved himself all would be well. Pryor nodded and rode on.

The heat was oppressive, and grew more intense as the afternoon wore along.

"We're goin' to get a storm," said Major North.

His prophecy was right, for around four o'clock thunder began its cannonading. Vivid flashes of lightning streaked rapidly approaching black clouds, driven before a mighty wind unimpeded in its dash over the plains. The whole sky grew dark as the sun was blacked out.

The Rio Kid ordered the train halted, and told drivers to stand by their animals. A stampede might be in order when the vicious storm broke over their heads. Tarpaulins were battened down and all waited the blow.

First came the violent wind, snapping at the canvas and shrieking through the wagons. It brought blinding clouds of dust, stinging the flesh, cutting off vision. The lightning was closer and the earth shook with the thunder reports. Startled horses reared and sought to bolt, but were held by their owners or others.

Big spatters of rain slanted upon the train then. But quickly this changed to hail, the stones opaque and white, and as big as pigeon eggs. They rattled on the Osnaburg sheeting, on the stretched canvas, on the hides of oxen, mules and horses, on the human beings forced to attend the stock. Mustangs shrieked and fought their holders. Even the stolid oxen objected to the bombardment.

The center of the violent shower passed, deafening them, the mighty lightning darting tongues of flame at their heads. The prairie was covered with hail but when the worst had torn by, sheets of rain fell, drenching the waiting people and all exposed equipment.

It lasted about half an hour but it seemed longer to the victims of Nature's whim. Soaking wet, stunned by the majesty of the elements, they began to breathe more easily as the sun returned to steam the earth, and the winds abated. They could see the nimbus clouds running southeast away from them.

But this was not the first such storm they had experienced. They had become accustomed to cloudbursts which would quickly flood streams usually fordable, and delay them. Sometimes the ripping winds were even worse than such swift blows.

The Rio Kid and the men in his charge checked up, repaired the damage, and the train marched on.

That night Celestino Mireles acted as commander of the guard. When the evening meal was over and the people relaxed before the fires for a time before turning in, the young Mexican approached the Rio Kid.

"Ees Fullhouse Watts again, General. He say he ees seeck. Yuh weesh me to make him stand guard?"

"I'll speak to him. He's been shirkin' all the way."

Pryor strolled down the line. Fullhouse

Watts traveled on his own horse and slept as a rule under a big wagon, rolled in his blanket. But it was the law of the prairie that every ablebodied man stand four hours sentry duty each second night.

The burly Nutcracker Lynch moved away from the Conestoga which sheltered Fullhouse as the Rio Kid approached. Watts was lying on his back, his head cushioned by his saddle.

"How about it, Watts?" said Pryor. "Yuh've taken yore tour only one night since yuh joined us."

"I'm sick," drawled Watts. "Told yore Man Friday so."

"How is it yuh're always ailin' when it's yore shift, but if there's a chance to cheat someone at a game yuh feel chipper?"

Watts' eyes narrowed. "Who says I cheat?"

"I do." It was just a surmise on Pryor's part, but he could tell from Fullhouse's manner that he was right. "Now get yore hoss and go on guard."

Fullhouse Watts stayed where he was, glaring. The Rio Kid stooped, seized him by the collar and yanked him up.

"Hustle! Yuh're keepin' better men than yoreself waitin'."

Watts swore and twisted around, but did not strike out or attempt to draw his pistol.

Pryor shoved the gambler along. Watts saddled his black and reported to Mireles. Such sentry duty was imperative, for no one could guess when marauders might attack, and wagon trains on the way to Santa Fe could be a windfall for robbers, with it being a long time before civilization learned of their depredations.

Slow wagons, laden with calico, hardware and gewgaws took eighty days going west. From Santa Fe, which had been American for only a score of years, came furs, buffalo hides, wool, gold and turquoise, taking as long in transit. With lighter loads the run east might require only half the time to reach New Mexico.

Into the unknown stretches of prairie, desert and mountains came trickles of humanity, linked by faint trails. Ploughs tore through sod, and grain was planted. The crack of bullwhips, groan of wagons, shouts, curses and prayers of men and women challenged the wilderness as the Southwest was invaded by its conquerors.

In all of Kansas, Nebraska, California, New Mexico, Arizona and Texas, an area larger than Europe, there were now not two million inhabitants. Railroads, as the Rio Kid like other men of vision knew, were the vital need of the new empire. But hardly fifty thousand miles of track had been laid in the entire United States and most of this, save for the new Union Pacific, lay east of the Missouri.

Jay Gould and Jim Fisk were playing with the destinies of a nation. They had their eyes chiefly on the populated areas of the Atlantic seaboard, and Western railroads were laughed at, refused financial backing. What the Southwest must have was iron to Santa Fe to open up the rich, unbelievably vast territories.

All this was strongly in the mind of the Rio Kid when, at Pawnee Rock, a towering butte on which travelers over the Trail marked their initials for later comers to read, the train stopped for two days. It was delayed by broken axles on two Conestogas.

Webb Daggett was steadily improving and, in the warm sunshine, he could limp around a little or sit on a folding camp stool, talking with Sari and Galusha Shannon, or with others in the party. His wound was healing but he still seemed weak, and the Rio Kid made no demands on a man who was recuperating from the terrific shock he had sustained.

Pryor himself kept busy, helping here and there, settling small frictions as personalities conflicted. The business of being captain of the caravan was an exacting one, calling for continued diplomacy.

The second day was hot, and the sky a clear blue. The Rio Kid recalled that Zebulon Pike had come past here on his famous journey into Spanish lands. Many another famous explorer, adventurer and soldier also had visited Pawnee Rock. It was a known point on the Trail, one of the few.

Steelhide Cass and Celestino Mireles had gone after buffalo beef, and Major Frank North had driven a flat wagon out to pick up the meat. Then keen eyes reported to the Rio Kid that riders and a carriage were approaching from the north, in the opposite direction from which the hunters had gone. And they were white men.

The Rio Kid rode out to greet the visitors who had sighted the billowing tops of the wagons drawn up in defensive array. On the front seat, beside the driver of the vehicle, was a friend Pryor recognized.

"Colonel Holliday!" he exclaimed. "What you doin' in this neck of the woods?"

"I might ask you the same." Cyrus Holliday, famed equally as Kansas lawyer, editor, and railroad builder, smiled, reaching out to shake hands as the Rio Kid leaned from his saddle.

"I'm takin' this wagon train through to Santa Fe, suh," Bob Pryor said.

"And we're making a preliminary survey for the Atchison, Topeka and Santa Fe Railroad," informed Holliday. "You know we've started laying track from the capital."

The Rio Kid grinned broadly.

"That's right. I saw it when I was there last month."

CHAPTER V
DEMOCRATIC VERDICT

Before Bob Pryor had moved on to Westport where he had been engaged to guide the wagon train people to Santa Fe, he had stopped in Topeka. There he had met Colonel Holliday. Everybody in that section of the country knew the colonel, who had been talking and writing and working for a railroad into the Southwest for the past decade. There had been long fights in Congress for land grants, and longer arguments for finances for the colonel's pet project.

All this the Rio Kid knew. Also, because the career of the colonel fascinated him, he knew that Holliday had been born in Pennsylvania. When he had graduated as a lawyer, he had married and hung out his shingle. A small local road had hired him to draw up a charter, and he had grown interested in rails. At twenty-eight he had come West, up the Kaw River, and in 1854 had set up a town on the south bank of the stream.

The Rio Kid grinned, recalling that Holliday and his friends had been so sure of their settlement's destiny that they had allocated twenty acres for the state capital! And Topeka, which meant "potato patch" in the local Indian tongue, had been made the capital within six years, largely through Holliday's efforts.

But none of this was a surprise to the Rio Kid. For he took pride in the fact that such men of faith made up his West.

In spite of all that men like Holliday had done for Kansas, though, matters there had not always run smoothly. Abolitionists from Pennsylvania had settled Kansas, for the most part, and they came in conflict with the Missouri Border Ruffians, who believed in slavery. It was civil war there in 1855, when the Ruffians attacked. Holliday had been made a colonel at the siege of Lawrence, and promoted to brigadier when he repulsed the enemy.

He had been Topeka's first mayor, and had served in the Kansas legislature, besides running his newspaper. Now he was known far and wide as a leader. A man to be proud of knowing, thought the Rio Kid.

But always Holliday had kept fighting for

the great idea of a railroad into the Southwest, one of the things on which the Rio Kid's own heart was set, though naturally he could do nothing about it actively. Holliday could — and had. Lack of money had not stopped Holliday; neither had ridicule.

He was past forty now, a man of reserve and dignity, tall and sturdy. Side-whiskers framed his pleasant face, although he was almost bald.

To the Rio Kid he was an upstanding figure of a man, neat and clean in heavy, uncreased trousers worn outside high, handmade boots, and with his silk shirt, initialed CKH in silver scroll, tucked in at his wide belt. A Prince Albert coat and a stovepipe hat lay on the seat beside him. He had removed them in the heat of the afternoon.

"You know Captain John Ellingwood, my chief surveyor?" Holliday asked the Rio Kid. "And this is Tom Peters, my builder."

Pryor shook hands, and nodded to the armed horsemen. They would, he thought, be a match for roving Indians.

The visitors entered the big camp, and Holliday and his companions were presented to the Shannons and others of the party who came clustering eagerly around.

All were delighted to see new faces, and to hear news from the East.

"Not many more wagon trains will run to Santa Fe," declared Holliday earnestly, when conversation had gone on for a time. "Soon everything will be railroads. Our road for one, will run out of Topeka across the vast reaches of Kansas, through Colorado and New Mexico, tapping the untold mineral wealth of the Rockies and meet the broad Pacific."

Some hid skeptical grins, others openly smiled as Holliday in fancy settled the Southwest with his iron rails. That such a thing could be possible was as yet unbelievable. But the Rio Kid, listening, saw visions and dreamed dreams.

Holliday ate supper with the Rio Kid and his friends — broiled buffalo steaks, coffee, pots of beans and hard bread, sweetened with molasses from crockery jugs brought in the store wagons. That night they sat before the campfires, and the colonel expanded his theme of the Atchison, Topeka and Santa Fe. The Rio Kid listened, intent and awed. . . .

Next morning the colonel took his leave, going back across the prairie toward the railhead. One thing the Rio Kid gathered from the railroad builder's talk was that Holliday had shrewdly figured that his road would intercept the great cattle drives up from Texas and so gain quick, lucrative business for the Santa Fe.

The Rio Kid led the wagon train on along the Arkansas. The river here coursed through deep beds of sand, and he chose to travel a few miles inland to avoid bogging down. They could move back in the evening for water. Pryor wanted to make as much speed as possible to reach Fort Dodge, staffed by a small force of United States troops which could assist the Trail travelers against the Indians.

On and on snaked the caravan, fighting dust and storms, patching equipment, tending those who were taken ill. Day followed day, a good run here, a bad run there.

It was not until after they had left Dodge behind that the Rio Kid grew aware of real dissension in the party. And he further realized that something would have to be done about that promptly.

When first he knew what he faced, they were nearing Cimarron Crossing. At this point they must decide whether to continue along the Arkansas on Zebulon Pike's route or strike southwest across the desert to the Cimarron River. To take the Cimarron route meant a fifty-mile run with no water except what could be carried or found in chance rain pools. No wonder that trackless waste was known as *Jornada del Muerte,* Journey of the Dead. It was a sun-baked, desolate trip and justly dreaded, for animals and men alike had perished from thirst in the arid reaches.

Before arriving at the Crossing, the Rio Kid called a council one evening. Galusha Shannon, Silas Gregg, a grave, bearded man of fifty, Jake Cochran, a stockraiser taking his wife and four children to settle in New Mexico, H. C. Hons, a carpenter by trade, accompanied by his bride, and Billy Eckert, a huge man who was an excellent black-smith were among the first to settle in the circle, lighted by a smoldering fire and by lanterns. Soon the McCoy brothers, traders and storekeepers, Al Boyd, mason, George Oaks, shoemaker, and the Warrens, a father and two sons moving their families to new land joined the gathering. More and more men appeared and took their places. The people of the wagon train acted on the democratic principle in arriving at decisions. The Rio Kid now would set the facts before them and let them vote on a choice of routes.

Pryor regarded the faces as they waited

for the opening guns of the council. Here were young fellows filled with enthusiasm and undaunted, and Civil War veterans a few years older. Here were men who had been taught caution, perhaps too much, by fate's blows. Several had fought under Generals Winfield Scott and Zachary Taylor during the invasion of Mexico in '48, when the United States, sparked by President James K. Polk, had seized the new lands.

The children had been put to bed and their mothers were watching over them as the husbands and fathers sat in conclave. Steelhide Cass and his sentries ranged about the hollow square formed by the great wagons. Close to the Rio Kid lounged Major Frank North and Celestino Mireles.

Webb Daggett sat between Shannon and Fullhouse Watts. Daggett had been cultivating Sari's father assiduously. In the background stood Nutcracker Lynch and several toughs who were his cronies, wagon drivers, for the most part, hired by members of the train.

Understanding human nature as the Rio Kid did, by this time he was fully acquainted with the character of each man in the caravan. Few were altogether good, and few entirely evil, with no saving grace. The average struck a balance and tried to show kindness, gratitude and helpfulness. Some, more endowed with decency than the rest, attracted friends easily. Galusha Shannon was such a man. Others had dominant vicious traits and they, too, could command followers who admired such ruthless strength.

All in all, these men of the wagon train represented a slice of America on the march, driven by the hopes and fears common to humanity, subject to the reactions of these urges. Mankind was a herd animal, the Rio Kid reflected, collecting in droves, swayed by mass emotions, blindly trailing a powerful leader.

The murmur of voices rose in the prairie night. A baby was crying in one of the wagons, and the warm south wind brought the mournful howl of a coyote. Pipes and cigarettes were burning and some of the men had brought along jugs of a fiery brew.

When they were all assembled the Rio Kid stood up and raised his arm for silence.

"Folks," he said, "I've called yuh together so yuh can say whether yuh want to take a chance on the *Jornada* or stick to the river. Yuh've all heard plenty about the run from the Crossin' to the Cimarron. There's no streams or lakes for fifty miles and that means the animals will have a tough time.

However, we've had a good many thunder-storms from the southwest the past week and I believe we'll find rainwater pools here and there.

"The north route through the mountains, especially Raton Pass, is also hard. With heavy wagons yuh make very slow progress at times over the rocks, and it's a good bit longer than by takin' the Crossin'. I've ridden both roads and if it was dry I'd say let's keep on along the Arkansas, but this time my vote goes for the *Jornada.*"

Nutcracker Lynch's harsh voice broke out in derisive objection.

"Yuh was on a fast hoss, Rio Kid, and it's a cinch to make fifty mile that way. But even without breakdowns we'd be three, four days in the desert. I made that run once and I swore I never would again. Wasn't only the oxen and horses had their tongues swole out black from their mouths, but strong men died from thirst."

There was an outburst of argument, some favoring one course, the rest the other. When it diminished the Rio Kid held up a hand.

"Anyone else want to chirp?"

Webb Daggett rose then. He smiled and his tones were clear, his argument persuasive.

"You folks saved my life," he said. "I was as good as dead out there when you came along. I'm not a regular member of this party but I feel like a friend and have yore interests at heart, so I'd like to have my say, if yuh don't mind. I've been a trader on the Trail and I know the *Jornada.* If we had no women and children with us I'd agree with our captain. But as Lynch points out the desert means awful sufferin' and the weaker will be first to feel it.

"The last train I was with on the *Jornada,* two died from thirst and three more went mad and run off into the sands. We lost five Conestogas, loaded with thousands of dollars' worth of goods, had to leave 'em broke down for we couldn't afford time to repair 'em, and around fifty oxen, hosses and cattle."

The Rio Kid smoked the quirly he had rolled. Daggett's speech rather surprised him, not so much the contents as the strength the man displayed. Daggett was much better, but had appeared to be still weak. He had been quiet during his first days in the caravan, so Pryor had not taken much time to sign the man up. Now he sought to revalue Daggett.

Galusha Shannon spoke up. He was, he said, in favor of following the leader's advice. Others sided with the Rio Kid, but there were more who were struck with fear at the description furnished by Nutcracker Lynch and Webb Daggett. Men with wives and children wanted to keep on the longer route where there was always water available.

When the show of hands was polled the vote was two to one for the mountain route.

The Rio Kid accepted the verdict amiably.

"All right, folks," he said. "We stick to the Arkansas. It's around a hundred and twenty miles to Bent's Fort, ten days' run if we don't hit trouble. Then we swing south and cross the mountains through Raton Pass, head for Las Vegas where the two main trails join for Santa Fe."

Though Pryor gave no sign of it, he was disappointed, for he had given a great deal of thought to this matter, and believed his choice the right one. As they had neared the Crossing he had carefully checked the rainfall and because there had been so much local precipitation he believed that the Cimarron Cutoff would have been passable.

This would have saved time and trouble. And once they had left the *Jornada del Muerte* behind they could have followed the

Cimarron River past Round Mound and Wagon Mound, thence to Las Vegas.

But the majority had ruled.

CHAPTER VI

CONFLICT

Next day the caravan sighted a large band of Indians watching the big train with hungry eyes. Major North and the Rio Kid studied the savages through fieldglasses and reached the same conclusion.

"Renegade Pawnees," declared North, who had tamed a majority of the tribe and knew them well.

But he also knew that among them were rebels who refused to live on reservations, and that these raiders hung around on the Trail, attacking small parties, or stragglers from stronger caravans.

Buffalo herds were everywhere and Steel-hide Cass and Mireles had little difficulty in providing fresh meat for the hungry travelers. Food, therefore, was not a problem, but weather was. On the flat expanses there was nothing to check the winds which held sway, blowing with unimpeded force for hundreds of miles. They had encountered several gales and knew the biting strength of the whirling air.

On a particularly hot afternoon the Rio Kid and Major North were riding at the head of the train when they noted a funnel-like black cloud to the southwest. They knew what that meant and Pryor at once stopped the wagons, picking the only available break, a long, low mound near the river. He ordered holders to stand by the animals and try to have everything battened down.

As swiftly as they worked, to have everything in readiness, the tornado overwhelmed them with breathtaking speed. The world darkened and winds preceding the funnel brought blinding dust. The storm's voice grew until the shrill insistence was deafening. Startled horses reared in the circling currents surrounding the heart of the tornado. The canvas top of a big wagon ripped loose with a report as sharp as a cracking rifle and the cloth quickly flapped to shreds.

For a half-hour Nature's majestic power once more stunned them, and then the disturbance passed, leaving the sun shining over the plains. They watched the black funnel recede. The murderous core had missed them by two hundred yards. It left an irregular, deep furrow in the earth where it touched.

They were soon on their way again. The ordinary life of the train was picked up and there was plenty of hard work for all hands.

Yet the Rio Kid noted a change in the mental atmosphere. There was a tenseness growing between members of the party, and he was aware of constraint on the part of many friends. Nor did it lessen as the days went slowly by.

Out in front one morning, with Frank North, Steelhide Cass and Mireles, Pryor spoke of it.

"It's Fullhouse Watts and that muleskinner Lynch," North said promptly, nodding. "I've seen it coming but didn't want to speak about it. They're settin' folks against yuh, Rio Kid. I been watchin' and aimed to tell yuh soon as I could."

Steelhide Cass said he had noticed the same thing and the Mexican nodded. All three agreed that the caravan was stirred by restlessness and uneasiness.

"I can lead these people as long as they want to be led, boys," drawled the Rio Kid. "Once we're through Raton Pass the goin' is downhill and easier. I figger we'll make it if luck holds."

But aggravating delays ate up precious time. One wagon after another developed trouble. A wheel would roll off, letting the heavy body down, stopping the entire caravan until repairs were made. Or a spring would go, which meant the same thing. It seemed as if an epidemic had struck the vehicles.

Nerves were growing frayed, and the Rio Kid checked several arguments and fights at the danger point. He knew now that Fullhouse Watts and Nutcracker Lynch were talking against him behind his back but neither man would stand up to him and face him down with an accusation of any kind.

The human beings in the moving settlement were subject to the usual emotions of mankind, swayed by the same reactions. So it was that on a fair, calm evening when the train had drawn up for the night, and dinner was being cooked over fires of smoldering chips, a spark which had been surreptitiously kindled, ran through the camp with the speed of lighted blazing powder.

A young man dashed past the Rio Kid, who lounged on the ground, nearly stepping on Pryor's hand.

"Hold up!" ordered the Rio Kid. "Where yuh goin' in such a hurry, Billy?"

Billy Dunn's eyes were bright with excitement. "Didn't yuh hear? It's gold! Gold! Come on!"

■ ■ ■ ■

Steelhide Cass was dozing in a blanket under a wagon, for he was due to take over the guard at midnight. Mireles was marshaling his sentries at the far end of camp. Major North jumped up and hustled with the Rio Kid to the spot to which Billy had run.

As though by magic, word had flashed to everybody and the entire train, except for a few women caring for young children, had gathered about Webb Daggett. The man who had been snatched from death in the desert stood at one side of Galusha Shannon's light rig. Fullhouse Watts and Nutcracker Lynch hovered close at hand.

"One side, and let me through!" ordered the Rio Kid. He pushed to the fore and faced Webb Daggett. "What's all this?" he demanded.

There was a challenge in Daggett's flecked gray eyes. The Rio Kid suddenly felt that he had never known the man at all, and that in this instant Daggett had snatched back the veil and showed his true character. The white scar puckered Daggett's left cheek and his eyelid twitched. He seemed fairly to grow in stature, and Pryor squared himself for a struggle with the tall, lean Daggett.

The man's bridgeless nose resembled a wedge of pale cheese. It had not browned as much as the rest of his face and stood out against the darker skin. His strong jaw was set.

Yet Daggett was too clever to close in a direct conflict now with the powerful captain of the train. He smiled, and made a deprecating gesture. His voice was even and gentle, and to those watching he must have seemed the essence of kindness and simplicity.

"I told yuh how grateful I was to you folks for savin' my life," Daggett said, in a clear voice. "But I did not tell yuh why I was out in the wilderness, alone, Rio Kid. I've thought it over, though, and have decided to reward yuh all. I own a map of a gold strike in the Rocky Mountains, not far north of the Trail. It's almighty rich, so there's plenty for us all. I'm willin' to lead my friends to it."

Daggett beamed and an excited cheer rose.

"So that's it!" growled the Rio Kid. He sought to comprehend Daggett's purpose. Men seldom publicly exposed such a secret if it was of any account. "Let's see the map."

Webb Daggett hesitated, then held up a

sheet of stained paper, which had been folded several times. There were marks on it, dotted lines and crosses, the usual figures expected on such a crude chart.

"Huh!" The Rio Kid deliberately turned his back on Daggett and spoke to the others. "Folks, gold strikes are happenin' all the time. Yuh must savvy that. Out of a thousand rushin' to a discovery, one may find enough to buy groceries. All yuh got here is Daggett's word and a few scratches on a paper. I contracted to take yuh through to Santa Fe and I aim to do just that, but yuh got to stand behind me. Once yuh're there yuh can form prospectin' parties if yuh've a mind to, but yuh better get there first."

Galusha Shannon had a grave word to offer. "The Rio Kid is right, friends," he said. "Our train should proceed to Santa Fe. Gold we are not sure of, but we are sure of good lands and a chance to earn a comfortable living in New Mexico."

Wiser heads agreed. The group around Daggett diminished and the more thoughtful of the party returned to where the meals were being cooked on the campfires. Without another word, the Rio Kid also stalked away.

The Rio Kid rolled in his blanket after

dark. Celestino Mireles was on duty, commander of the guard thrown around the hollow square, so safety was assured. Pryor was quickly asleep, as the stars made a canopy over the camp.

It was past midnight when he jumped awake at the sounds of wild confusion. Men were shouting and hoofs made the ground tremble. He thought it might be an Indian raid, until he heard the cry:

"Stampede! Stampede!"

Leaping up, ready to whistle for Saber, in order to help check the runaways, he saw a revolver flare, and a breath later the sharp report reached him. A man screeched.

The Rio Kid darted along the line of bulky wagons.

"Who's that?" he bawled.

Tinder had been tossed on the fires and the night breeze whipped up a reddish glow. Hurrying figures crossed the camp to assist in pursuing the missing stock. Horses and even stolid oxen had galloped off, stirring up dust.

In his eyes at that moment was a second stab of flame, and now he could see that the marksman was at the rear of a big Conestoga. The bullet whizzed past his ear, too close to be a mistake.

"Hold it!" he warned. It might be an excited friend who, in the darkness, believed him an enemy.

He stumbled over a writing figure in the black shadow cast by the wagon, and dropped to his knees beside a wounded man. He recognized Shelby Keith, a young fellow who had been among Mireles' guards for the first watch. Keith gripped a Navy revolver in his hand. He lay on his back, moaning. His horse stood a few paces away, with dropped rein, dancing with nervous excitement at the noises.

"I'm hit!" gasped young Keith. "Dyin'!"

"Who shot yuh?" demanded the Rio Kid. His left hand, which rested on Keith's side, was wet with blood.

"Nutcracker Lynch," gasped the sentry. "He started — stampede. Look out!" Shuddering possessed Keith's gaunt frame. He rose to a sitting position, whispered "Mother!" and fell back.

The Santa Fe Trail had claimed another victim. The Rio Kid, bent on revenge now before thought of anything else, left the dead Keith and moved around the wagon. No one was around, for members of the night guard had ridden far out on the plain in an attempt to circle the animals, vital to further progress of the caravan.

Lynch had eluded Pryor in the moments the wagon train captain had been at Keith's side. But the grim Rio Kid continued his search, poking in dark spots under vehicles or behind equipment.

On the other side of the hollow square a sharp voice hailed him. The Rio Kid recognized Webb Daggett's tones.

"Is that you, Rio Kid? What yuh after?"

"I want Nutcracker Lynch," replied the Rio Kid coldly. "He just shot Shelby Keith."

The Rio Kid stepped close to the high wheel of a Conestoga where he would not offer too easy a mark, for he was unable to see Daggett. And all trust in the man was gone now.

CHAPTER VII

THE LURE

Canvas rustled at the back of the wagon and the Rio Kid guessed that Daggett must be inside, although Daggett had said nothing more as several seconds had ticked away. The hackles at the base of the Rio Kid's neck prickled as they often did when danger was at hand. He had felt the same sensation during the battle, and on the Frontier in perilous times.

At last Daggett jumped from the tailboard and came around the Conestoga.

"Take it easy, Captain," he drawled. "Don't get upset about that fight between Keith and Lynch. It was fair. Keith drew first and Lynch fired in self-defense. I saw it all."

Daggett loomed before him and the Rio Kid slid along the side of the wagon toward him.

"Where's Lynch now?" he asked, holding himself in.

In the firelight, Daggett's eyes glinted.

"Don't get excited," he said. "Lynch surrendered to me. I promised I'd put in a word for him."

"I savvy."

Hails between riders after the runaways, the voices and stirrings of men and women in the camp, broke the quiet of the prairie night. Then the Rio Kid's sharp ear caught a faint sound from the wagon.

"Out of the way, Daggett!" he ordered sharply. "I want Lynch!"

"Wait a jiffy!"

Daggett blocked him, and the two faced one another challengingly. As Daggett refused to budge, the Rio Kid seized the man's wrist and whirled him around, slinging him from his path. But Daggett did not draw a gun, though the Rio Kid expected that and was ready for it. Instead the tall man folded his arms in dignified silence as the wagon train captain stood by the tailboard.

"Come out of there, Lynch!" snapped the Rio Kid. "Jump down with yore hands in the air!"

"Don't shoot!" growled Nutcracker. "I'll come if yuh promise not to gun me."

"I won't fire if yuh behave."

Nutcracker Lynch showed after a brief

interval.

"I got no gun on me," he said gingerly. Plainly he was fearful of the Rio Kid. He had his blunt hands over his matted head as he squatted on the high tailboard, hopped to the ground. "It was a fair fight, like Daggett says, Rio Kid. Keith meant to down me."

The ox driver's squat, powerful figure bulked in the reddish glow from the fires. Daggett kept his arms folded but the Rio Kid watched him from the corner of his eye. Then Major North came suddenly around the Conestoga, to back up the wagon train boss.

"Lynch just shot Shelby Keith, Major," explained the Rio Kid.

"Put him under arrest," advised North, his voice cool.

"That's what I aim to do," Pryor said grimly.

Knowing that, North would watch Daggett, the Rio Kid walked over to Nutcracker Lynch, who drew back in alarm as if prepared to resist. But Pryor caught him and with a trick learned in the Army whirled the heavy fellow around.

"Keep yore paws off me!" shouted Lynch, and then made the mistake of fighting back.

The Rio Kid lunged forward, lithe as a

panther, and his fist stabbed into Lynch's eyes and nose, while he avoided the teamster's clumsy counters. As Lynch bent back from a punch Pryor brought up a knee and the driver was doubled up, his breath knocked out. He went down from the sudden shove against his shoulder and the Rio Kid fell on him hard.

But the Rio Kid was taking no chances. He knew that Lynch had a knife in a sheath and a pistol hidden under his shirt. With slashing blows from his own Colt barrel the Rio Kid forced him to quit struggling, and relieved the killer of his arms.

Pryor stood up, panting. Other men who had heard the commotion had arrived now. Fullhouse Watts and Galusha Shannon were among them.

"Yuh got no right to kill him!" cried Webb Daggett, as the audience increased. "I tell yuh it was a fair fight."

"Shut up, Daggett!" ordered the Rio Kid. "I warned Lynch about pullin' a gun on anybody in this party. We'll tie the cuss up and give him a trial in the mornin'."

Lynch was secured and placed in a wagon under guard. . . .

It was dawn when the dusty, sweated horsemen who had pursued the stampede returned, driving most of the runaway horses before them. The oxen had not stampeded far, and were already back in camp. However, the train would be delayed again for most of the day for the men must rest, as must the weary draught animals as well.

Breakfast was prepared as the light grew stronger over the shallow valley of the Arkansas. Tempers were short, because the night stampede had broken the sleep needed by the hard-working travelers. The Rio Kid could hear the voices of young fellows talking together as they squatted in groups, drinking from tin cups filled with steaming coffee.

Gold!

The word kept cropping up, spoken with the tense excitement it always touched off in mankind. There was plenty of gold in the mountains, it was whispered, fortunes waiting for all to pick up. Routes were traced in the dust by shaking forefingers or sharpened sticks. The fever had spread with blinding speed and it destroyed the reasoning ability of sober-minded men who before had sought only land.

Webb Daggett was late in showing himself. But now he had many friends among the wagon train folk, those interested in the precious mine of which the map he owned showed the location. And Daggett had promised to lead them to riches. Daggett was a benefactor!

The Rio Kid called the men together after the meal. When the sun was above the horizon, Nutcracker Lynch was put on trial for the shooting of Shelby Keith. Daggett was there, to speak for Lynch.

"It was self-defense," insisted Daggett, again and again.

"Keith drew first," growled Lynch sullenly. His faced showed the marks of the punishment he had taken from the Rio Kid. "Keith, he went off half-cocked, boys. Got excited in the stampede and figgered I was an Injun, I reckon. I didn't aim to kill him — just tried to pertect myself."

The Rio Kid was the chief accuser.

"Keith told me that Lynch started the stampede last night," he said grimly, "and that Lynch shot him down. I s'pose Keith was close in and spied Nutcracker as he loosed the hosses. Why did yuh want to hold us up again, Lynch?"

The ox driver refused to answer. He glared in black fury at the Rio Kid. Webb Daggett jumped into the breach.

"That's loco!" he cried indignantly. "Lynch had no reason for startin' a stampede. It don't make sense."

"I'm in favor of hangin' the prisoner, gents," declared the wagon train captain firmly. "He's a killer."

Pryor fully realized that the camp had become divided into two factions. Behind him stood Major North, Steelhide Cass and Mireles and other men not easily swayed. On Daggett's side were Fullhouse Watts and his kind, as well as plenty of decent men who had been blinded by Daggett's plan to mine gold in the mountain.

Arguments were bandied backward and forward, and the verdict finally arrived at was banishment from the train. Lynch was to pick a horse, but he could not have any firearms. A bag of food was furnished him.

Webb Daggett, who had acted as his champion, shook hands with Lynch and spoke with him just before Nutcracker rode off on the back trail along the river.

In the four days that passed after Nutcracker Lynch disappeared in the dusty haze, and another man had taken over the piloting of Silas Gregg's heavy wagon, the train snaked along only fourteen miles. When a wheel suddenly rolled off a loaded Conestoga it sometimes took hours to jack up the body and make the repair, and again an epidemic of such breakage seemed to have struck. Tension was mounting between the opposing groups, and every hour lost increased this.

North, Steelhide Cass and the Rio Kid talked it over on the fourth evening as the prairie night closed in.

"We've come a long way and the axles are wearin'," observed the Major. "Still, they don't look too bad, Rio Kid."

Bob Pryor nodded. "I reckon we didn't get rid of our troubles when Nutcracker Lynch was run off, boys. We'll check up on every wagon before we start mornin's."

"I figger most of the breaks are due to somebody tamperin' with the wheels," Steelhide Cass grunted. "But who's fool enough to want to hold us back?"

The Rio Kid shrugged. "I've thought it out mighty careful. Daggett is winnin' over more and more folks to his way of thinkin', and all he needs is time. Wish I could catch him workin' on a wagon. But I s'pose Full-house Watts and others are in on the game, too."

There were many vehicles in the big train, though, and when the wind clouds scudded over the moon and stars it would be easy for a man hidden under a wagon to remove a key nut or bolt. Nevertheless, the next day the Rio Kid and his lieutenants carefully inspected every piece of rolling stock. Naturally more time was lost, and the sun was well up before the caravan heard the order to march.

By then the Rio Kid had reached the conclusion that if Daggett was trying to run the show in an underhand manner he was doing it cleverly. Pryor had been unable to trap the man. Daggett and Fullhouse Watts were not so crude as Nutcracker Lynch and they would not rise easily to bait.

That afternoon Webb Daggett set up a cry which was relayed along by all within hearing.

"The mountains! There they are, boys!"

"Gold! Gold!"

The Trail, after leaving Bent's Fort, swung southwest through the divide by way of Raton Pass, and now in the northwest distance showed bluish peaks, subsidiary ranges of the mighty Rockies, outlying sentinels thrust to the sky.

The get-rich-quick fever waxed stronger until wavering souls decided to join the mine faction as the goal actually came in sight.

That night they camped on the north side of the narrowing river, where a cooling breeze off the mountains dispelled the day's heat. Talk buzzed in various groups as the evening meal was prepared and men rested after the labors of the day's run.

Bob Pryor was eating his supper with North and Mireles when Galusha Shannon sought him out. The Rio Kid noticed that Shannon, whom he greatly admired, walked slowly, though since he had joined the caravan sun and wind had bronzed his lined face and he seemed stronger.

Shannon sat down by the Rio Kid.

"Captain," he said, "I've come to tell you something. Webb Daggett has asked me for financial backin' for that mine of his, in return for a share of the stock. I'd value your opinion."

"I don't like Daggett and I don't like gold mines that ain't proved," declared the Rio Kid firmly.

"You don't believe in it, then." Shannon sighed. "I've been feelin' much better lately, and I've thought maybe the mountain air might complete the job of healin' my infirmities. But I don't know. Anyhow, Daggett's soft-spoken about it. He only put it in the form of an offer."

"Daggett's not what I'd call stupid," drawled the Rio Kid. "If he was I'd have got rid of the cuss long ago. But I can't find a reason to toss him out."

"Here comes Daggett now," said North. nudging Pryor.

Chapter VIII
GAMBLER'S GAME

Half a dozen members of the camp were with Webb Daggett. They proved to be a delegation sent by a large number of the people to sound out the boss of the train about Daggett's gold mine.

Daggett was the spokesman. He kept his voice down, but it was clear and firm, and his flecked gray eyes were riveted on Pryor's. There was power in Daggett, a ruthless sweep challenging the Rio Kid.

"Why don't I pick a fight with the wolf and shoot him?" wondered the Rio Kid.

But he knew he could not, unless Daggett chose to make it gun to gun. The Rio Kid was not a bully, nor did he ever kill except for good and sufficient reason. He had never shot a man unless his own life or that of another was in obvious danger, and even then he would always give fair warning.

"We're here to ask yuh to lead us to the mountains, Captain," Daggett was saying.

"We want to reach the gold mine. We'll need food and supplies while we work and there's plenty in the wagons. Game can be shot in the hills as well."

The Rio Kid studied the man.

"Yuh've done a real job, Daggett," he finally said. "Yuh've got these folks pantin' to follow yuh. I don't savvy what yore real aim is, but I'll never fall in behind yuh."

Daggett's face darkened. His anger at the Rio Kid's outspoken criticism was plain. For an instant Pryor hoped that Daggett might break and show his true colors, offering him, Pryor, a chance to destroy this dangerous opponent who had obtained such a hold over the caravan folk.

But Daggett gave no opening, holding himself in.

"I don't savvy what yuh mean, Captain." His tone was injured. "I'm grateful to yuh all for savin' my life and only want to try and return a favor. That's the only reason I'm givin' away the secret of my mine."

The men all listened attentively, their expressions weighing what each leader had to say. They would retail these opinions to others in the camp.

"I was elected captain of this party," the Rio Kid reminded them all. "And so far we've gone along all right. As long as yuh follow me I'll stick to yuh. Like I told yuh. I aim to run this train through to Santa Fe as contracted. Not all the gold in the Rockies will change me. That mine's a lot farther off than it looks and even if there's metal in there, which I doubt, it will be a long, hard job before it's out of the ground. Yuh haven't got any proper equipment and yuh haven't got the experience. Once in New Mexico it's up to you folks what yuh do, but while I'm headin' yuh we stick to the Trail."

That decision was final, leaving no doubt about the Rio Kid's stand. Daggett's fists were clenched and his scarred eye corner twitched as the eye narrowed, the puckered cheek obeying the pull of the cords. But he said not a word. Turning on his heel he strode away.

The delegates were thoughtful as they split up, to spread the Rio Kid's ultimatum through the encampment. He was still boss, and most of them remembered that for many weeks they had looked to him for guidance and protection.

Dark fell and with it quiet. The Rio Kid was alone with his close aides.

"Yuh sort of told Daggett off," chuckled Major North. "Mebbe yuh'll scotch his game yet, whatever it is."

The Rio Kid was not so sure. He shook his head. "He's a sly rascal, North. He's got somethin' up that sleeve of his. I hope to figger it out sooner or later. . . ."

For two days the wagon train made good time on the Trail. Breaks were fewer and over twenty miles were clocked off by the slowly turning and creaking wheels. The mountains had turned from bluish to brownish as they came closer, and ahead could be made out the faint outlines of greater heights. They were in Colorado now, and Bent's little outpost was but a few days run to the west.

Then late in the afternoon of the second day, while the Rio Kid and Major North were scouting ahead of the train for a suitable camp site, Galusha Shannon's carriage broke down. The seasoned wood of the right axle snapped and several wheel spokes split. Sari and her father were spilled out on the grassy way and the startled horses bolted, dragging what was left of the Rockaway from the Trail across a rough area. Jutting gray rocks reduced the vehicle to firewood.

When the Rio Kid rejoined the caravan he found Sari and Galusha riding with Silas Gregg, the merchant. Their packs were stowed in the rear of Gregg's Conestoga.

As they were setting up camp for the night, a thunderstorm rolled off the mountains and drenched them. The air was cool and the fires, started with tinder kept dry in the waggons, smoked as dampness pervaded the wood and chips. The sky remained dark, because of a layer of clouds, the blackness broken only by the limited circles of reddish glow around the blazes.

Steelhide Cass and his guards rode restlessly around the hollow square, ready as always for attack if one should come.

The Rio Kid and North lounged on their blankets by a dying cookfire. Mireles was off by himself, napping, since he must take over the guard at midnight.

"Things have been quiet lately," drawled North, after a long, thoughtful silence.

"Too quiet," the Rio Kid said. "I'm waitin' for Daggett's next move, to tell yuh the truth."

"Mebbe yuh're right, at that," North agreed.

After a time North joined Celestino, rolled in his blanket under a nearby wagon. The Rio Kid sat up, taking it easy and rolling smokes, aware of the dying bustle in the encampment as weary travelers were overcome by sleep.

A lantern burned down the line and the quiet figures of men playing for high stakes showed in the faint light as they squatted about the spread blanket serving as a table. The fires were low, limiting the range of vision more and more, while the high, canvastopped Conestogas cast dense shadows. The Arkansas softly purled in its bed and the shrill pipings of insects and tree frogs filled the background.

This peace was broken as a man cursed loudly. Two of the gamblers jumped up as an altercation quickly began. The Rio Kid hastily rose and hurried toward the spot to check the fight.

It was Fullhouse Watts' game that was going, of course. He always found time for one. The Rio Kid had forced Watts to stand his guard tours but even so Watts had managed to shirk his full share of work, in favor of gambling. Dapper and smooth, his crisp mustache bristled and his dark eyes glowed as he squatted on his hams, looking silently at the captain of the wagon train as the Rio Kid approached.

Watts was not one of the participants in the furious argument. That was between two ox drivers, coarse fellows who had been friends of Nutcracker Lynch, and who were dogeying one another across the blanket, hands to their knife hilts.

"I'll cut yore cussed liver out and feed it to the fish!" bellowed one. "I seen yuh slip that ace from under the blanket!"

"Yuh lyin' sidewinder, yuh'll never get near enough to touch me," boasted his opponent, a hulking brute with a black beard and huge shoulders. "I'll tear yuh to pieces and toss yuh to the buzzards. I dare yuh to take one step this way!"

The air was blue with their profanity as the Rio Kid stepped between them.

"Break it up, boys," he ordered. "Go turn in. Yuh're keepin' the whole camp awake. We got a long run tomorrow."

The men subsided, glaring at the Rio Kid and at one another. But neither of them made an attempt to come to grips.

"Can't we play a while longer, teacher?" asked Watts sarcastically.

"Move!"

The Rio Kid had only contempt for the gambler, whose type he had met too often on the Frontier. A shove sent Fullhouse reeling and Watts shrugged, picked up his cards and money and went off. The rest split up and Pryor, after making certain the two belligerents had gone in different directions, strolled around the hollow square for a last look before turning in.

Most of the people were asleep, but here and there someone stirred. A few quietly walked through the encampment. But this was the usual state of affairs, and all appeared to be well.

The Rio Kid paused to speak with Steelhide Cass who rode up and saluted him.

"Nothin' in sight so far," reported Cass. "It's mighty dark out there, but I got a double guard strung where they'll do the most good."

"Bueno." The Rio Kid nodded, and went on.

Reaching his roll he shook out a blanket and lay down, his head pillowed on his saddle, the packs spread as a shield. The sky was still black and the quiet of the night was a soporific.

But as he was drifting off to sleep he suddenly started awake. A group of men had approached him, their heavy boots thudding on the earth. He rose to face them and they stopped, silently watching him in the faint light from a dying fire.

"What's up?" he demanded.

A bony man of fifty, with watery blue eyes and a graying beard, was pushed to the fore. He wore corduroys and a flannel shirt, a soft hat and black boots. Known as "Uncle Hy" Reiner, he was noted chiefly for his ability to drink anything alcoholic that was in sight. He was traveling to Santa Fe with his niece and her husband, a couple emigrating to the Southwest for homestead land and a new freedom.

The Rio Kid had taken scant note of Reiner except to classify him as a vacillating character with a penchant for strong liquor, useless but harmless. It was rumored that Uncle Hy had a fat wallet about which he would boast when in his cups.

Reiner began to accuse the Rio Kid in a shrill voice, pointing at him with a crooked, shaking forefinger.

"He done it! I seen him! He thought I was snoozin', but I watched him slip my poke from the pack. There's eighteen hunderd in it."

"Yuh're loco," snapped the Rio Kid. "Yuh've been soppin' it up again, though where yuh got enough I don't savvy."

The liquor supply had run low several days before, and there were only a few quarts left, conserved for emergencies.

The Rio Kid sensed real trouble, though, and quickly gauged the men backing Reiner, who was in a state of nerves. One was Fullhouse Watts, which didn't surprise the Rio Kid, but another was Silas Gregg, whom the wagon train captain knew to be an honest and upright man. The others were drovers, who had been in the poker game that evening, two more were serious, hardworking family men, and friendly to the Rio Kid.

"I kept my eyes shut and snored some," piped Reiner, tremulous but not intoxicated. "The Rio Kid come and busted up the game and then he slipped near me and stood for a minute to make shore I was asleep. He stooped and got my wallet, then he hustled on around the camp. I didn't dare say anything for fear he'd kill me."

"I can't believe this, Rio Kid," said Gregg soberly. "Reiner woke me and told me what had happened. I saw yuh crossin' over, and yuh stopped to speak with Cass."

"Yuh're lyin', Reiner," growled the Rio Kid. "At best yuh've made a mistake. I'm no thief, and I didn't touch yore money."

"I seen yuh take it!" insisted Uncle Hy. "Shoot me if yuh want to, but yuh stole my roll! Never thought yuh'd pull such a low trick!"

Men were rousing as Reiner's penetrating voice rose over the camp. Major North and Celestino came on the run to join the Rio

Kid. Galusha Shannon and Webb Daggett hurried up, and swiftly others arrived on the scene to find out what the trouble was. Steelhide Cass, commander of the guard, rode up and sat his horse, watching and listening.

The moment was tense, and pregnant with trouble.

CHAPTER IX

SPLIT

For a time the Rio Kid did not fully realize the depth of the trick his enemies had concocted to destroy him. The soul of honor and honesty himself, a man who would never condone a base act, the charge, to him, seemed ludicrous. But as the men of the caravan crowded around and Uncle Hy repeated his story, Bob Pryor found himself in a ticklish position. He knew that thievery was not uncommon in such caravans, and that all too often men succumbed to moments of weakness. He had never imagined, though, that he would ever be so suspected.

Fullhouse Watts spoke then, his voice a challenge.

"Boys, yuh savvy I ain't a pard of our captain. Like Reiner says, Pryor may gun me for what I'm goin' to say, but I feel I got to tell it. We were playin' cards when the Rio Kid busted up the game. He roughed me some, and I was on my way to turn in

95

when I happened to glance back. I saw this here Rio Kid squattin' by old Reiner. The light wasn't too good, but I'm shore he took somethin' from Uncle Hy's pack."

"I seen the same thing," promptly declared a drover, who had been in Fullhouse's poker party.

The Rio Kid thought fast. He recalled how the spat between the poker players had drawn him to the game. Now Watts and his cronies accused him of theft. Could that argument have started just to get him there?

Another man chimed in — Lewis Tate, a carpenter by trade, a strong young fellow who had always backed the Rio Kid.

"I saw just what Gregg saw," he said. "The captain walked past my wagon a while ago, that's all."

The majority waited, confused, unwilling to believe such a story about their leader. So far Reiner had been corroborated only by rather disreputable members of the train.

Webb Daggett pressed forward.

"Perhaps there's been a mistake," he said mildly. "It might have been someone who looked like the Rio Kid. To tell the truth I was lyin' under Tate's wagon, I was awake. I saw a feller I thought was the captain speak to Watts, then move to where Reiner was bunked. Shorely if he's innocent, the Rio

Kid will let us search him and see he hasn't got the wallet on him."

Pryor shrugged. "Go to it. Only stand back, Daggett, and you, too, Watts. Let Shannon do the searchin'."

All trusted Galusha. He stepped in, carefully checked the contents of the Rio Kid's pockets. He found a wallet, but Uncle Hy shook his head.

"That ain't mine. Mebbe he hid it in his packs."

"Look in 'em," ordered Daggett.

Galusha Shannon stooped and emptied the nearer saddle bag. A well-worn black leather pocketbook fell out and Reiner gave a cry.

"There it is! I told yuh so."

A concerted gasp ran through the gathering.

Shannon was astounded. His bearded jaw had dropped. It was a terrible moment. Webb Daggett's carefully controlled voice broke the stunned silence.

"Yuh mustn't blame him too much. Any hombre yuh meet will weaken once in a while. Mebbe the Trail wore out our captain, who's no better than the next man. He figgered he could sneak out Reiner's poke and lay it to somebody else who don't set up to be a tin idol. He slipped for a moment, that's all."

"Dry up, Daggett," snarled the Rio Kid, as the man he now realized was his enemy condemned him with weak excuses. "That wallet was planted in my bag."

Yet even as he said that, he realized how feeble the words were. Every man so trapped offered the identical alibi.

Fullhouse Watts smiled in derisive triumph, and Daggett seized the whip hand. In the rear of the gathering a couple of Watts' bunch stealthily drew revolvers. Steelhide Cass saw that, and threw up his cocked carbine.

"Hold it! I'll drill the first man who aims a gun."

Mireles and North sided the Rio Kid. Shannon stood where he was, his grave face etched by anxiety. But most of the men drew back from the wagon train captain who had led them thus far on the dangerous Trail.

"Take it easy, Cass," snapped Daggett, face twitching as he glanced around. "Arrest the Rio Kid! Drop yore guns, Pryor. Yuh'll have a fair trial."

Webb Daggett loomed over them, facing the Rio Kid who, shorn of his reputation, was likewise shorn of his power to command.

"No, Daggett," said the Rio Kid. "I don't surrender to such as you."

Daggett stood in front of the Rio Kid and his flecked eyes studied the captain's grim face. It was plain he wanted to disarm the Rio Kid, and then dispose of him, but though Pryor had only a few fighters remaining by him, they were known as the best shots and most determined souls in the party. If a shooting bee broke out Daggett would be the first to catch lead.

"Boys," Daggett said in a loud, harsh voice, "yuh're welcome to take him if yuh want to. I speak for myself when I say I've had my fill of the Rio Kid. We'll elect a new captain for the rest of the trip."

The Rio Kid regarded the hostile eyes about him. The confidence in him of the men he had led was shaken. He had believed they were for the most part his friends, but they had been turned against him.

"I won't say anything more except that I didn't touch Reiner's poke," he drawled. "And yuh've been fooled by a mean trick. I'll ride at dawn, as long as yuh feel the way yuh do. Anybody who wants to come with me is welcome."

"I'm with yuh, Rio Kid," said Frank North, and Mireles stood beside his trail partner, scowling at Daggett.

Galusha Shannon put a hand on Pryor's shoulder.

"I believe in our captain," he said. "I'll go with him."

But Shannon's good heart was known to all and it was thought he was only seeking to befriend the Rio Kid in his time of need.

"Mr. Shannon!" cried Daggett. "You can't ride far on hossback. Yuh'll be far better off in the protection of the train."

Steelhide Cass moved his horse over on the Rio Kid's side.

"Count me in," he growled.

Daggett and his cohorts walked away, leaving North, Mireles, Cass and Shannon with the Rio Kid. The caravan had turned against their leader.

Shannon offered his hand to Pryor.

"I know they're wrong and you're right," he said. "You couldn't do such a thing."

"Thanks." The Rio Kid nodded. "I appreciate yore trust. But what Daggett says about yore ridin' with us is sense. Yuh can't fork a mustang for long, and Sari couldn't make the run. We'll head for Santa Fe in the mornin', and you'll be there soon."

North and Celestino were anxious about the Rio Kid's safety. A crowd of armed men had collected down the camp, with Webb

Daggett in their midst. Others had gone to spread the story to their wives, and to oldsters who had not been in the gathering.

After a while Galusha Shannon returned to his bed. But Steelhide Cass and Major North maintained a watch as the Rio Kid snatched a nap to renew the strength he would need.

It was not long before the gray dawn broke. The Rio Kid rose, washed, and crammed his few belongings in his saddlebags and ate breakfast with North and Mireles. When the horses had been cinched up the cloudiness had blown over and a red band in the east bespoke a hot, clear day.

The camp was quiet, men speaking in subdued tones. The Rio Kid was being avoided, let strictly alone, but Daggett. drinking coffee with the new leader and his lieutenants dared not attempt to take the Rio Kid.

Shannon appeared with Sari. "Rio Kid, I'm with you in spirit all the way!" cried Galusha. "But you're right, I couldn't ride far. I'd only hold you back. And Sari couldn't stand such a trip, either."

The Rio Kid nodded. He knew that was true. Shannon had a lame back and could sit a horse for but a short period. And Sari was not an experienced horsewoman.

Slowed by an invalid and a girl, the Rio Kid's small party would prove easy prey to red marauders of the Trail. Shannon did not even have his light carriage now, but was dependent on Silas Gregg for transportation.

Saber stood waiting, as were North's big horse and the young Mexican's elegant mount.

"Come on," ordered the Rio Kid. "If Daggett starts shootin' somebody will get hurt!"

"Rio Kid!" That was Steelhide Cass. "I want to go with yuh. But I can't."

Pryor frowned. "They'll kill yuh if yuh stick here."

"You go along, Andrew," ordered Sari. "I'll meet you in Santa Fe."

But Steelhide was held by his love for the girl.

"I've got to stay with the train," he said doggedly. "I'm needed here."

A man had the right to make up his own mind, and the Rio Kid understood fully. Steelhide Cass' decision was no reflection on his bravery, for he was willing to face death, anything, for Sari.

Cass shook hands with North, Mireles and the Rio Kid, and the three rode out of camp, picking up speed westward on the

Santa Fe Trail. Bent's Fort was not far ahead for horsemen on such fine mounts. They could get through Raton Pass with much less difficulty than the cumbersome wagons and be in Santa Fe within a few days.

Catcalls and howls, a few pistol shots, followed the trio but there was no attempt made to stop the Rio Kid. Perhaps Webb Daggett was glad to see his rival leave the train.

Before they were out of sight, the Rio Kid looked back over a hunched shoulder. The wagons were drawn up as they had been for the night. Steelhide still stood there, with Sari and Galusha, staring after them. All three waved as they saw the Rio Kid turn. Others watched as the discredited wagon train captain and his companions picked up speed, but no one else cheered them on their way.

The Rio Kid rode for about a mile in grim silence. Then a terrace slanting from the river cut off the wagons from sight.

"That's that," he finally said to North. "I s'pose Daggett will swing 'em off to his mine."

"Let 'em stew in their own juice," growled Frank North. "They're fools."

"Some are fools, Major," replied the Rio

103

Kid gravely. "But others are just the decent, regular run of folks. They've had the wool pulled over their eyes and yuh can't blame 'em because plenty have fallen into the same old trap."

"I been thinkin' it all over," said the major. "Daggett must have bought Uncle Hy Reiner or scared him into accusin' yuh. They hid his poke in yore pack while yore back was turned."

"Yes." The Rio Kid nodded. "It's plumb plain to me it was a carefully laid plan to get rid of me. Fullhouse Watts and his pards drew me that way by raisin' a ruckus so that even my friends had to admit I was close to where Reiner was. You saw the rest of it."

"We should have gone after Daggett and Watts before they got it rollin'," declared the angry North.

"If we'd started firin' there might have been a bunch of people hurt, includin' women and kids," the Rio Kid remonstrated soberly. "And goin' off half-cocked would have made us look even more in the wrong. Let's hope that Shannon and the cooler heads can talk the party into makin' Santa Fe."

The Rio Kid and Major North were a few paces ahead of Celestino Mireles, whose keen eyes swept the horizon.

"General!" he called sharply. "See what ees!"

Chapter X

BANDITS!

Quickly the Rio Kid and North pulled rein, slowing to stare in the direction indicated by the young Mexican. They were north of the river where the valley swept up a rocky slope to the first crest of hills, fringed by a ragged line of timber and brush that stood out against the lightening sky.

Rider broke from this screen, wild horsemen with blackened faces and eagle feathers bobbing on lowered heads. More and more burst into the clear, tearing down on the three horsemen and whooping it up as they sighted them.

At first glance they would be taken for savages with naked, bronzed torsos and features smudged with charcoal or berry juice. Some had bound their hair with rattlesnake skins or bright strips of cloth, while the rest sported hats.

"They look like Injuns," observed the Rio Kid coolly, as he pulled his carbine from the socket under his leg and cocked the weapon. "But some of 'em are whites. What you say, Major?"

North was one of the best experts in the country at identifying the numerous tribal markings. He was in no doubt at all.

"They're white men fixed up as savages," he said. "One thing's plain — they're after us."

Bullets began to shriek over them as the attackers pulled triggers at long range. Spurts of earth kicked up as slugs thudded into the ground, and one that ricocheted from a rock whistled with an ominous, protracted sound and splashed into the water.

"Let's go!" cried the Rio Kid. "There's fifty or sixty of the cusses! Trail robbers, I reckon."

"S'pose we slow the rascals down," drawled the Major. "They're too allfired eager for their own good."

The Rio Kid was game and snugged his carbine to his shoulder. For really fine aim with that weapon it was necessary to pull up. He did, and drew bead on an oversized figure stripped to the burly waist. The powerful black stallion the big man mounted was far superior to the ordinary plains mustang and had carried him twenty yards to the fore, A black Stetson was strapped so low it pushed his ears off at right angles, and he kept bellowing to the surging bunches of killers to hurry up.

Not wishing to hurt the black if he could help it, the Rio Kid sighted high. Frank North's steady rifle crackled at almost the same instant and the leader of the attackers straightened in his saddle as his hat flew off. The stallion jumped and whirled off course, nearly unseating the huge gunslinger, who dropped everything to cling to the horse's flying mane.

Sunlight gleamed on his bald pate. The man had no hair at all and the side of his head seemed as perpendicular as sheer cliffs.

Major North uttered a startled exclamation. "I savvy him! That's Squarehead Bull Fanning. I had a run-in with the cuss last winter in Nebraska! Once yuh see that top of his yuh never could mistake it!"

"Bull Fanning, the bandit?" shouted the Rio Kid. "He was raidin' from Dakota to Texas, I heard tell. Wonder what he's doin' so far West?"

Mireles was firing steadily and a couple more from the Rio Kid and Major North slowed the pursuit. The attackers in front, who had been so eager to catch them, seemed to lose interest as lead slashed flesh.

A man dropped out, hugging his shoulder, and another began yipping, with a bullet-hole in his leg. A mustang crashed head over heels while its rider landed hard on all fours and stayed there, shocked to the core. "Squarehead Bull" Fanning kept rubbing his sheening cranium. Had the lead missile that had whizzed by ranged an inch lower, Fanning knew he would have been lying dead on the hill.

Lines of outlaws spurted out from the timber now, and the three men who were being attacked knew it was time for them to move on before they were circled and killed at leisure by the overwhelming forces. They sent rapid shots at the enemy and picked up speed, sticking to the beaten Trail and alert for possible raiders who might have been sent ahead earlier and posted to ambush them as the main band pursued them.

"Did yuh note that squat devil close on Fanning's left?" called the Rio Kid to Major North. "He had a mighty familiar look."

"I didn't," confessed North. "I was busy studyin' Fanning."

The Rio Kid kept glancing back. The sun was up behind them and the day clear. Nature smiled over the Santa Fe Trail, smiled with benign sweetness, as savage men sought the kill.

Squarehead Bull Fanning, no longer up front but driving his bunch from behind, maintained the chase. The Rio Kid held the rear, with Mireles checking the unwinding road and Major North on the side toward the Arkansas. The Rio Kid was not worried over the possibility that Fanning might attack the wagon train for such a party, properly captained, would be able to beat off the bandits.

Suddenly the Rio Kid sang out: "Major! I believe that hombre I spoke of is Nutcracker Lynch! I just had a real good peek at his side face."

"Yeah? That may explain why they're so hot after us. Lynch may have hooked up with Squarehead and laid for yuh."

They didn't know. But one thing they did know. Death snapped at their heels as they drove on. . . .

Back at the caravan they had left behind, Steelhide Andrew Cass was well aware that in remaining with the wagon train he was asking for death. He had consistently stood with the Rio Kid, had fought Nutcracker Lynch, and had openly opposed Webb Daggett and Fullhouse Watts.

But Cass could not desert Sari. He had a

cold courage which never quailed, and he was not afraid. But for the sake of the girl and her father he had decided he would knuckle down as far as possible to Daggett, and always keep in mind his chief aim — to protect the Shannons.

He did not have long to wait before the enemy came to try him out. The Rio Kid, Major North and Celestino were scarcely out of sight on the Trail before Daggett, Watts and a couple of tough drovers rounded a Conestoga and faced Cass.

"I want to talk with yuh, Steelhide," said Daggett, beckoning to the frontiersman. "Step over here."

The men who faced Cass were watchful and heavily armed. One of the ox drivers was carrying a sawed-off-shotgun across his hairy arm in a most suggestive manner.

Cass obediently moved toward Daggett, his stalwart figure relaxed and easy in his buckskin garments, his curly dark hair catching the sunlight from under his hunter's cap.

His face was clear and guileless as Daggett stared at him with twitching gray eyes.

"Yes, suh?" replied Cass. "What can I do for yuh?"

Daggett regarded him for a moment. The

big camp was stirring about them as the travelers discussed the Rio Kid in excited groups. Some could not believe that their former captain could be guilty of theft. Others accepted the evidence and the witnesses' stories. Hot coffee and the morning meal were being consumed, pipes and cigarettes lighted for a bit of relaxation before the day's march began.

"Yuh've been a friend of the Rio Kid," said Webb Daggett. His voice had an imperious ring. Plainly he considered himself the new chief of the caravan. "Do yuh think that he stole Reiner's poke?"

Cass shrugged. "Shore looked like it. To tell yuh the truth, Daggett, I been thinkin' more of somebody else than of the Rio Kid."

Daggett nodded. He reached his conclusion as to Cass.

"I won't bother yuh as to that," he said, "so long as yuh behave yoreself and take orders. Savvy? There's plenty of work for yuh but if yuh kick up I won't give yuh a second chance. Is that plain?"

"Mighty plain. Yuh want me to keep on huntin' for meat?"

"No. I'll assign others for that. Watts will tell yuh my wishes if I'm not on hand. Take over Silas Gregg's wagon for the time bein'."

Daggett did not disarm Cass, as he found

him tractable and willing to obey. In spite of the fact that another man had earlier been pointed out as the new wagon train captain Daggett spoke as though he himself had already been elected captain, and shortly thereafter this assumption proved correct, at a meeting called in camp.

Daggett was chosen to lead them to the mountain gold, the few dissenters overwhelmed by the enthusiasm of the get-rich-quick adherents. With the Rio Kid out of the picture, Webb Daggett easily triumphed, and it was voted that the caravan turn north into the hills.

Distant gunshots from the west were heard, but ascribed to buffalo hunters or roving Indians.

The sentinels Daggett had thrown out did not report that there was any threat to the train.

The wagons packed, Daggett, with Full-house Watts at his side, led the march along the Trail. Steelhide Cass sat on the box of Gregg's heavy Conestoga, handling the ribbons controlling the yokes of oxen drawing it. He could watch Sari Shannon, who was riding with her father and Gregg in Gregg's carriage.

Daggett had quickly taken over. He had

relieved those he trusted of their duties in the train so they might ride as guards and be at his beck and call. These men for the most part were toughs, drovers and mule-skinners who had fallen in with Watts and Daggett, who would work for anyone who paid them.

But the majority of men in the caravan willingly followed Webb Daggett, because they hoped to win riches in the gold mine.

CHAPTER XI

STRANGE FATE

In the afternoon the caravan led by Webb Daggett turned off the Santa Fe Trail and slowly slanted off on a grassy slope. The mountains rose before them and they could see a deep gap which Daggett, studying his map, announced was their goal.

There were bearings on the chart which Daggett kept to himself. But it was understood that all were to share in the mineral wealth once they arrived at the spot. The fever again had risen and men could scarcely contain themselves until they should reach the diggings.

Toiling to the top of the first slope, a grassy plateau opened before them, deep in waving grasses and studded with wild flowers of various hues. The horsemen in the lead of the caravan broke a path through the growth. The iron-shod wagons, crushing a trail, sank into the virgin earth.

When they stopped for the night, Steelhide Cass took care of his oxen, turning them in with the herd to graze, then went to join Sari and her father. He was content so long as he could be by the girl's side. He helped her prepare dinner, and after eating sat and talked until it was time to turn in. . . .

The train resumed its progress once more after breakfast the next day. Daggett had full control now and his wishes were followed out without question. Cass kept quiet, did as he was told, and in return he could be with Sari. He knew that Daggett was evil, but his hands were tied because of his desire to protect the Shannons.

On two occasions other drovers, men whom Cass was sure had gone over to Daggett body and soul, tried to draw Cass out. In low tones they criticized the new leader, cursed him to Steelhide, and sought to discover his true feelings, but he parried these attempts to trap him.

"It's all right," Cass kept saying. "We'll make it. I reckon there's gold in the hills. That's what interests me."

It took the slow wagons four days to reach the spot which Webb Daggett had indicated, though it had long been in sight. The region was breathtakingly lovely in its wildness. A boiling white mountain torrent rushed through a rocky bed at one side of a gulch. The eastern wall of this cleft had eroded so that there was plenty of room for a camp, and grass carpeted the ravine floor, with stunted timber patching it here and there. There were trout in the pools carved in the brown rock by the rushing waters, and there was game in the hills and wooded areas.

Reaching this garden spot, Webb Daggett stopped his horse and turned, raising his hand high in the evening air. The sun was out of sight behind the peaks towering beyond but there was still plenty of light. When the vehicles had drawn up and the people were listening, watching, Daggett cried dramatically:

"This is the place!"

Hoarse cheers rose from dusty throats. Men threw their hats and caps in the air and some fired off their guns in joyous acclaim.

"Hurrah for Cap'n Daggett!" bellowed a teamster, and the tall leader was rousingly applauded.

Some of the younger fellows, unable to wait longer, threw themselves from their saddles or from the wagon seats and hurried to the edge of the stream, hunting for gold nuggets. Others, of steadier disposition, unhitched the draught animals and began setting up camp, before permitting their emotions to seize control.

That night everyone gathered around a blazing fire of dead pine limbs which had been picked up along the bank. The voice of the torrent echoed from the rocky walls and Webb Daggett, addressing the meeting, had to speak with all his force to make himself heard.

"Folks, we're here, mighty close to the mine," announced Daggett.

"Where's the gold?" called someone. "Nobody found any in the creek."

"I'm comin' to that," replied Daggett. "Yuh chose me captain, and I have yore best interests at heart. The first thing we must do is build a settlement, for we'll be here a long while. There's plenty of pine and spruce above that can be rolled down to this point where cabins can be put together.

"We'll need meat, and our hunters can lay in sheep and antelope, salt it down. I aim to send a pack train to fetch more flour, salt and such provisions, so when our supplies run out we'll have a new store. Minin' takes time. Yuh can't expect to pick up a fortune in a few days and dash off with it."

Steelhide Cass silently digested Daggett's words. As yet he did not understand what

Daggett's aim was in bringing the train to the mountains. He had begun to believe that perhaps there was gold around, but that Daggett wanted help in mining it. So far, though, no gold had been seen. But Daggett was in the saddle, riding high, and those opposing were in such a minority that his supporters could crush them at any time they so desired.

"But the gold?" insisted Al Boyd, the mason. "How about the gold?"

Daggett frowned. "One thing at a time, boys. I purposely fetched yuh here to this ideal townsite. Why, some may even wish to make it their home for life. When we're set up I'll lead yuh to the mine. Otherwise yuh'll go off half-cocked and wear yoreselves out before yuh have provided food and lodgin'."

There was some grumbling at this, but others thought it sensible. As Daggett said, mining took time; months, even years. Shelter must be had. In the winter snow would fall heavily in the mountains.

Early next morning all set to work under Daggett's direction, Cass among them. He was as strong as a young bull and a willing hand as he axed down pines, trimmed off the branches and cut the boles to the proper lengths. Chains hooked to yoked oxen helped drag the materials to the town site and the spaces between the pine logs were chinked with reddish mortar made from a clay bank and water. Tarpaulins and tents eked out one-room cabins. With the carpenters and masons in the party, within three days a startling transformation had taken place in the valley. A settlement nestled there, with people dwelling in it.

Under Daggett's command a larger building had been erected, and the wagon train captain himself had quarters off it. A crude bar ran along one wall and benches, stools and slab tables filled the room. A long sign over the entryway, made from a white pine slab and a can of black paint which had been brought in one of the wagons, proclaimed:

DAGGETTVILLE
Bar & Hotel — W. Daggett

Also, at Daggett's insistence, Silas Gregg had unpacked his Conestoga and set up his store of goods. The wagons had been parked close together against the eastern cliff, and the horses and oxen were useful in the construction work or for hunting.

Steelhide Cass was putting the finishing touches on the Shannons' home, with Galusha and Sari assisting, when he looked down and saw a large band of horsemen slowly filing into Daggettville. At their head rode a huge man in black leather pants and shirt, a tall Stetson with a hole through its crown canted on his great head. The chin-strap was loose in its runner, and the great figure jogged easily up and down with the motion of his handsome stallion.

He wore twin Colts with silver filigree in the walnut stocks, the cartridge belts crossed over his barrel chest. Mexican spurs adorned his creased boots and he held a carbine across the horn of his expensive, hand-carved saddle.

Behind him came more than fifty riders. Tall and short, fat and thin, in leather and buckskin, with tall hats, flat hats, even a scattering of coonskins. Some were bearded, others clean faced save for the day's stubble. But they had one thing in common — each was heavily armed.

The creak of leather mingled with the clinking of metal as they slouched in their saddles, filing into the gulch.

"Sari!" cried Cass. "Here comes Nut-cracker Lynch!"

The ox driver, who had been exiled from the train, was in the van. Sari, Galusha and Cass stared at him and at the fierce faces of his companions. The Shannon cabin was one of the first at that end of the ravine and the huge leader of the oncoming outlaws noticed the pretty girl. He straightened in his saddle, raised his black Stetson and grinned.

As he exposed his cranium its unusual shape could be observed. He was completely bald and the sides of his head were straight up and down. Cass felt an inward shock. He had never happened to encounter Squarehead Bull Fanning, but had seen pictures of the bandit on circulars, in a number of Kansas and Nebraska settlements, and recognized him at once.

Fanning passed, and Lynch came abreast. The ugly driver glared with fury at Cass, who stood his ground. A slim, darkskinned outlaw with an upturned black mustache and sideburns, and who wore Mexican clothing, swerved out of line and gallantly swept off his steeple sombrero, bowing low to Sari. A pair of whiskey bottles hung from his saddle-horn, one on either side and he had been drinking from both to keep them balanced. His face was flushed from liquor and heat.

"Senorita!" he exclaimed. "How beautiful! How may I serve yuh?"

Bull Fanning glanced around as Cass pushed between Sari and the Mexican bandit. The huge chief's flat cheeks flamed with swift rage and he dug a spur into his great stallion and was upon his amorous follower in a flash. A burly arm snaked out and the thick quirt attached to Fanning's wrist cracked, wrapping around the bandit's shoulders and stinging him with leaded tip.

"Back in line," snarled Fanning. "I'll rip yore hide off if yuh don't behave. I'll do the pickin' in this shebang."

The drunken outlaw who had accosted Sari shrank from his chief and hurried into his place, head hanging, while his companions snickered. Others eyed Sari, but there was no further annoyance and the new arrivals rode on and pulled up before the saloon, where they dismounted to stretch their legs and smoke.

Webb Daggett appeared in the doorway and Bull Fanning, Nutcracker Lynch and a couple of other bandit lieutenants went inside.

"Why, Daggett seems to know them!" exclaimed Galusha. "And they look like outlaws."

"That big hombre is Bull Fanning," Cass said grimly. "He's the worst raider on the Frontier. They say he rules his bunch with an iron fist and the quickest Colt of 'em all."

Shannon's jaw set and he started toward the saloon. Sari caught his arm.

"Father! Where are you going?"

"To talk to Daggett. How can he be friendly with such bandits?"

"No, please!" begged Sari, holding him back with desperate strength. "They'll kill you!"

"I don't fear death," declared her father.

"But you can't leave me. What will happen to me? At least wait until the outlaws are gone."

Cass was all ready and eager to accompany Galusha. Sari had to plead with both.

"And you, Andrew! You mustn't take such chances with your life! They would have shot you if Fanning hadn't acted when he did. I saw Lynch loosening his pistol. He hates you. Can't you see that?"

Cass had made it his policy to avoid all trouble unless he was forced to act to protect the Shannons. Alone he could do little, for Daggett, Lynch and Bull Fanning had overwhelming power. He dropped back as Sari spoke, though it was reluctantly.

Fortunately Galusha Shannon also heeded Sari's plea.

"All right, Sari," he gave in. He added

stubbornly: "But I'm goin' to talk to Daggett just as soon as he's alone."

The outlaws hung around, drinking and smoking, eating what they could buy at the little store. The main saloon was filled with armed men. Some tended their mustangs, rubbing them down, letting them drink at the brook.

The people who had come in the wagon train were scattered. Women and children around their new homes, and the men were either at work or off on the slopes after logs. A number of the bandits ogled the younger women but made no attempt to annoy them. Evidently Fanning had ordered them, also, to behave.

The fresh mountain air carried on it the odors of frying meats, sheep and antelope steaks. Uncle Hy Reiner, a favorite of Daggett's now, was at the rear of the saloon, cooking over wood fires for Daggett and the guests.

Since Reiner had accused the Rio Kid and helped Daggett dispose of the former captain, Daggett had been most friendly. Cass had his own ideas about Reiner. He was more than ever convinced now that Daggett had bribed Uncle Hy in order to destroy the Rio Kid.

Chapter XII

DESPERATE SOULS

Late in the afternoon, the workers returned to their homes, weary from their heavy tasks. They were thirsty and hungry, ready for the suppers which had been prepared for them at the many shacks. Some of the men dropped in at Daggett's bar where they mingled with Fanning's riders.

Sari served supper to her father and Cass. It was a good supper, for on the Trail she had quickly become adept at turning out a tasty meal with scant materials. She had something besides a Dutch oven to cook on, too, for Steelhide had built her a stone hearth with metal grids. Also he had almost finished contriving a baking oven behind the cabin.

Dark had fallen before Bull Fanning lurched from the lighted saloon. He was full of whiskey and his voice bellowed profane commands, echoing from the mountain walls.

"Hosses, boys, and foller me, cuss it!"

He was a rowdy, given to heavy carousing, a stupid beast in some ways, but in others shrewd, and tough enough to command the riffraff of the Frontier.

He rode out of the settlement, his bunch behind him.

"Now I'll go talk to Daggett," announced Shannon.

"Won't you wait till morning, Father?" begged Sari.

"Here comes somebody," warned Cass, as a man loomed up on the path silhouetted against the saloon windows.

"Shannon!" a voice bawled. "The boss wants to see yuh!" It was Uncle Hy Reiner, come with the message.

Galusha patted Sari's hand. "Stay here," he said. "I'll find out what he wants and be right back."

"Go with him, Andrew," begged Sari. "But please be careful."

Cass trailed after Galusha who was following old Reiner on his way back.

Cass paused in the entrance. There were a few men drinking at the bar, among them Nutcracker Lynch, who had remained in town. Shannon crossed to the open door of Daggett's quarters and Steelhide, ignoring the lowering Lynch, followed Shannon.

127

Daggett had two rooms off the saloon. In the smaller one were bunks. The larger was furnished with crude seats and a slab table on which stood tin cups and a couple of empty bottles.

Daggett had changed greatly since joining the train as a wounded, helpless victim of Indians, and who had been befriended by the Rio Kid and the rest of the wagon train people. Daggett now had grown aloof, showed a dark, fierce vanity, and his voice was imperious and short. His bridgeless nose was the same, though, as was the scar which puckered his left cheek. He wore a plain shirt, black pants and boots, and a revolver was thrust into his belt.

"Good evenin', Galusha," he greeted. "Glad to see yuh. How do yuh like it, now we're gettin' settled?" Daggett had always treated Shannon with a certain deference. He glanced at Cass and nodded. "Set down, Steelhide. Yuh built the best cabin in town and yuh're doin' fine work."

"Obliged," said Cass quietly.

He took a three-legged stool in the corner and Daggett seemed to accept him as he turned to talk with Shannon at the table.

"I need yore help, Galusha," began Daggett. "I've got a big proposition here, but it will take financial backin'. I savvy yuh have credit in Eastern banks, and that's what's required. And if you come in, others like Gregg and Cochran will toss what they got in the kitty. Yuh've got a lot of influence."

Galusha Shannon shook his head. He was greatly disturbed, and had been holding his feelings in through the afternoon and evening.

"I always speak my mind if it seems right, Daggett," he said, "and there's something more important than money or credit right now. I was astonished to see you friendly with that outlaw, Fanning. And Lynch is right outside in the bar!"

Daggett frowned, regarding the indignant Shannon.

"Yuh can't be too particular in a spot like this," he said. "Do yuh realize Fanning could wipe us out if he had a mind to? He'd do it, too, at a word."

Steelhide Cass caught that veiled threat, and cold sweat stood out on him. It was all right for him to defy death and torture himself, but he suddenly saw how completely helpless were the people who had been led here by Daggett. With Fanning as an ally — if he was — Daggett held the whip hand, and could enforce any edict he chose to issue.

"Why do you need such financin'?" asked

Shannon. "If there's a rich placer gold mine in the vicinity it can be opened by hard labor and with hand tools."

Daggett assumed a frank manner. "I'll lay my cards on the table. I don't know of any gold around here. But I have a carefully made map of other deposits which will prove as valuable as gold, or even more so."

Shannon leaped to his feet.

"Then you tricked our friends into comin' here! You lied to us!"

"Set down — take it easy. Hear me out. Nobody's goin' to get hurt if they do as they're told. You don't need to work. Yuh can loaf along as my pardner. I've been mighty decent to yuh and want to stay the same. The thing of it is, this whole gulch is thick with copper, seventy to eighty percent ore, accordin' to the assays. That's why we're here. It's worth a big fortune. They use the metal in stringin' the telegraph wires and in the great Atlantic cables they're layin'. Cartridge makers got to have it as well, and right now there's a huge demand for it."

Galusha Shannon regained his control. He wished above all the probe to the bottom of Daggett's devious mind, and restrained himself.

"Very well," he said thickly. "Keep talkin'."

Daggett was willing. He had everything worked out in detail. The astounded Cass listened with dropped jaw and as Daggett spoke on, many matters which had been puzzles to him became clear.

"Minin' copper on a large scale calls for machinery and plenty of labor," declared Daggett. "We got the workers, and we're set for a good start. I aim to open the deposits with pick and shovel. This new railroad, the Santa Fe, which Colonel Holliday is buildin', will be forced to make Daggettville a stop. A spur will handle the ore and we might build our own smelter."

"How did you discover this metal?" inquired Shannon.

"Through a map a dyin' pard gave me. The rest I worked out, and I've thought of everything. After Nutcracker Lynch left the train he filed the claims for me, and started a pack train this way with tools and supplies."

"Also sicked Bull Fanning on us," thought Cass. But he kept his mouth shut.

He could see now why Daggett had disposed of the Rio Kid, and had been so insistent on swinging the caravan to the mine. The epidemic of delays, breakdowns and stampedes, fitted in. Aided by allies

131

such as Fullhouse Watts, Lynch and Uncle Hy Reiner, Daggett had carried through his scheme and was now proud of his vicious triumph.

Galusha Shannon had confirmed his rising suspicions. He rose, drawing himself up to his full height as he spoke emphatically.

"You're an evil man, Webb Daggett," he accused. "You've played with the lives and fates of my poor friends. In the mornin' I intend to call a meetin' to inform them of what you've done. I doubt if you'll get many volunteers from among them for your copper mine."

Daggett drummed on the table with his long fingers.

"I don't need volunteers," he finally said. "They'll work. I'm offerin' you a pardnership, and yuh're a fool to refuse."

Steelhide Cass feared that Daggett might kill Shannon for defying him. He would have stopped Shannon, if he could, but he knew the attempt would have been useless.

"I intend to start for Santa Fe as soon as I can buy a wagon!" Galusha cried. "The Rio Kid was right. We should never have left the Trail."

Perhaps Daggett hoped to win over Shannon later, for the boss of the new town made no further argument. He permitted

Shannon and Cass to leave the saloon.

That night Steelhide Cass hid himself in the rocks above the Shannon cabin and kept watch. He soon became aware of stealthy riders in the ravine and to the south where the plateau opened out. Any number of times he tightened his hands on his rifle, ready to fight for Sari and her father. But no one sought to force a way into the little shack and the gray dawn finally broke, a mist rising from the noisy mountain stream.

The Conestogas and other vehicles which had made up the train still stood in the park. But as the light grew, Cass did not see the horses and oxen which usually grazed on the grassy flats.

After breakfast Galusha Shannon called the wagon train folk together. Here were people who had come such a long journey into the wilds. The McCoys, traders, were big fellows with brawny shoulders. There were Al Boyd, the skilled mason, and George Oaks, the shoe maker. The Warrens were present, and Silas Gregg, grave of mien and a peer of Shannon. Cass knew them all, their characters and the strengths and weaknesses of each man.

It had been spring when they had left the Missouri. Now the summer was in full sway.

■ ■ ■ ■

Webb Daggett stood leaning against the side of the saloon, watching them. At one side of him stood Nutcracker Lynch; at the other was Fullhouse Watts. Uncle Hy Reiner and several ox drivers who had openly thrown in with Daggett did not bother to join Shannon's gathering.

Women and children were around. Sari stood in the cabin doorway with the fresh light glinting on her thick hair as she listened to her father, when he began to speak.

"Friends," Galusha Shannon said, "we have been tricked. There's no gold here — only copper, which belongs to Daggett. He brought us here to work his mine, and to gain financial backin' and power."

As Shannon explained the situation, some men grew dejected, while others burned with quick anger against Daggett.

"String the cuss up!" shouted a young hot-head.

"No!" Shannon raised his steadying hand. "We'll pack up and move on to Santa Fe as we should have done in the first place."

Steelhide Cass was keeping an eye on the surrounding terrain, and he saw riders turn into the gulch around the bulge of the reddish bluff to the southeast. Bull Fanning's bunch.

"Watch out!" he warned, and men gripped their pistols and rifles as they eyed the approaching outlaws.

Fanning was not with them; only a lieutenant in charge of the dozen men. They pulled up within hailing distance and the bandit in front raised his hand in a gesture of peace.

"Hey, folks! Yore hosses and oxen were all run off last night by a bunch of Comanches! We tried to come up with 'em but had no luck."

There was awe-struck silence for a moment. Everyone realized the import of those words. Without draught animals they were immobilized and all knew it.

Daggett's voice startled them.

"Every man drop his gun and raise his hands!"

The stunned, angry people looked behind them. The saloon bristled with gun muzzles thrust from windows and from the corners of the building. Bull Fanning stepped from the front door and moved into the open space beside Webb Daggett. The huge outlaw chief cradled a shotgun in his arms and wore his fancy pistols.

It would be a massacre if the wagon folk

tried to fight. Flying lead would slash women and children as well as men. The hopelessness of their situation broke upon them cataclysmically. They lacked means of leaving the isolated community! Daggett was lord and master!

Steelhide Cass was perhaps the most experienced fighter of all the men aligned against Webb Daggett. Cass had been hardened on the Frontier and through Indian torture. He was furious and would have gone against Daggett and Fanning singlehanded had he not long ago decided he must live in order to protect Sari and Galusha. He put down his carbine and raised his hands with the rest.

Daggett and Fanning, with half a dozen aides, walked among their prisoners, careful how they moved. Pistols, knives and rifles were collected, the men of the settlement disarmed. This accomplished, Daggett spoke again.

"Nobody will get hurt if yuh obey. I need yuh here for a while, and I want workers for the mine. Shannon told yuh there's no gold, but the copper's a rich lode. I'll give credit slips for the time yuh put in and yuh can buy at my store and the bar. My hunters will supply fresh meat. I aim to make this a goin' proposition."

Bull Fanning bulked at Daggett's side. It seemed evident now that Daggett controlled him and the gunmen who followed him.

Daggett turned away, but swung back.

"One thing more. Don't try to sneak out nights, anybody. There's a bunch of Injuns not far off. Same ones who stole the animals." He winked at Fanning and went back toward the saloon. . . .

For an hour Daggett left the captured caravan people to talk it over. Then he sent Lynch a message.

"Every able-bodied hombre will work in the mine," growled Lynch. "Hustle. Fetch a canteen and somethin' to chaw on pronto!"

Chapter XIII

WARNING

Galusha Shannon and several other elderly men were permitted to remain home, but the rest were herded up the ravine. Steelhide Cass, plodding toward the mine site, understood why Daggett had let him survive. It was because he had proved to be a valuable worker.

Such workers were necessary, he saw, when they arrived at the spot indicated. The copper lay just beneath the surface, with an oxidized outcropping here and there. In a short time Cass, bronzed torso bare and running with sweat, was swinging a pick, breaking off chunks of the stuff.

Daggett, Lynch, and other overseers were on hand. Back at the saloon, Fullhouse Watts was in charge, and Fanning lounged with his boys in the shade.

It was hard labor in the summer sun, and that first day was but the beginning of what seemed to become interminable toil. Hands blistered and cracked, but as day followed day, men grew hardened and their weariness when night came was not so unbearable.

A pack train pulled in. Daggett had said he had ordered Nutcracker Lynch to direct supplies to the gulch, after Lynch had been banished from the caravan. Now the pack train had arrived. Tools, and barrows, and whiskey in barrels, as well as a few luxuries, reached Daggettville.

The town finally took on the existence of any such mushroom settlement. The saloon stayed open day and night, and Fanning's men caroused there almost continually. Daggett was piling up copper and ore, biding his time. Eastern capital would eventually come in and the mine, the town, would make him a king. The complaints of his victims would count for little in the lawless wilderness, and within a few months Daggett would no longer need their help, anyway.

On a bright morning as the captives started for the diggings, one of the Warren boys was brought in, slung over a bandit's horse. Daggett called the impressed workers together. They stared at their dead friend.

"Pore Billy tried to sneak out and run away last night," said Daggett, with mock sorrow. "The Comanches got him. Look at his head."

Quincy Warren, Billy's father, was choking with grief at sight of his dead boy. A rough job of scalping had been done on Billy, who had been shot through the head and body as well. Of course everyone was sure that Billy had been caught by Fanning's sentries. It was with saddened, depressed hearts that they dragged themselves off to their forced work.

That evening as old Galusha, Sari, and Cass were eating, Shannon said in a low voice:

"Andrew, do you believe you could escape by yourself?"

Cass stared into Galusha's burning eyes. Shannon, Cass knew, had reached a point where he preferred death to further indignities heaped on himself and his friends. Steel-hide kept his voice down.

"I think I could make it, but I hate to leave you and Sari. I'd have to steal a hoss, though."

"No, Andrew, you mustn't try it!" objected Sari. "Look what happened to Billy Warren."

"I'd go myself but I wouldn't have the slightest chance," said Shannon. "You're the one man who might succeed, Andrew. This is unbearable. You must have seen Lynch beat Rafe Green this afternoon when Green was too sick to work."

"I saw it." Cass nodded grimly. "It's gettin' tougher."

"Daggett has threatened Gregg and Cochran with torture if they refuse to sign credits they own in the East over to him," Shannon said tightly. "And I can't hold out much longer. It's not loss of the money, but I fear Daggett may destroy most of us in order to protect himself, once he gains his way."

"I'll go tonight," Cass said promptly. "Yuh reckon I should head east or west for help?"

"West," ordered Shannon. "Try to find the Rio Kid and tell him what's happened."

After dark Steelhide Cass turned in behind the cabin as usual. The saloon was lighted and raucous voices came from it. Fullhouse Watts was running a game there. Whiskey barrels stood on log racks, broached with wooden spigots.

Mounted sentinels patrolled the southern mouth of the gulch and the widening plateau beyond. The moon was not yet up. The sky was powdered with stars, but the towering cliffs cast dense shadows.

Steelhide Cass was ready. He wore moccasins and leather pants, and had bound his hair with a kerchief which Sari had given him. Dark mud blackened his face and torso so there would be no sheen. He crept toward the bluff. Long ago he had noted the crevice in it, and this was now as black as ink. He slipped between the rocky lips and began to work his way up.

It was after midnight by the time Steelhide crouched on the lower, outer bluffs. He had come around by what Daggett had considered an impossible route. Only a trained frontiersman could have negotiated it. Steelhide would have been elated at his success, except that in the back of his mind was anxiety over what Daggett might do to Galusha and Sari when it was found that Cass was gone. But he had the faculty of concentrating on the task before him, and did, realizing its importance.

With patience learned from the Indians he waited, several feet above the general level of the plateau. After a while a rider came along and stopped, whistling through his teeth. Before long another appeared from the direction of the gulch and the two spoke together.

"Got a light?" asked one.

"Shore. Wait till I roll a quirly."

The flare of the big match as they lighted up showed Cass all he needed to see. They were Fanning outlaws, and one was the hellion who had accosted Sari the day the band had arrived.

"Slow, ain't it?" yawned the other man. "Two hours of this a night is more'n a plumb plenty, Pablo."

"*Si*," agreed Pablo.

The dark bandit was on a long-legged buckskin gelding and Cass liked the mount's looks. The buckskin would be fast, and these sentries had just come on duty so the horse would be fresh.

The other gunslinger rode off toward the settlement. Pablo sat his saddle, the red tip of his cigarette marking him for Steelhide. Cass dared not push his luck too far, but he must have a mount and be out of the vicinity before dawn, or they would run him down and kill him.

He launched himself through the air, the ruby circle of burning tobacco his target. He could not afford a miss. He landed behind Pablo and his left arm circled the stunned bandit's throat while his right gripped the wrist. The buckskin jumped and plunged at the sudden shock, but Cass had legs trained to hold on.

He heard the crunch of cartilage as his concentrated force choked Pablo. His free hand smashed attempts by his foe to turn on him or draw knife and gun.

"Hey, Pablo! Are yuh all right?"

That was the other sentinel. He had caught sounds of the scuffle and was coming back.

With desperate strength, Steelhide Cass twisted Pablo's neck, hurled the dying bandit to the ground, and was off. . . .

A pack mule laden with an antlered buck and smaller game followed the Rio Kid and his two comrades of the chase, Major Frank North and Celestino Mireles. To the south they sighted the little station of Bent's Fort, where they had spent the past two weeks.

After shaking off Bull Fanning's band the three had reached Bent's, tired and showing wear and tear. Their horses had needed a rest and so had the men. The mountain air had seemed beneficial to North, easing his asthmatic breathing. Hunting trips into the hills had served to pass the time and the handful of men at Bent's, now a stage station and an oasis on the Santa Fe Trail, appreciated the fresh meat.

The Rio Kid was much interested in the history of Bent's Fort. The place had been built between 1829 and 1832 by the three brothers Bent — William, Charles and George — assisted by Ceran and Marcel St.

Vrain, mountain men and trappers. It stood on the north bank of the Arkansas. Trail travelers, after leaving it, would swing south, negotiate the rocks of Raton Pass and reach the Purgatoire River.

Once Bent's Fort had been a major trading center, and a gathering place for Americans, Mexicans, and American Indians. Kit Carson and young Dick Wootton once had hunted meat for guests who swarmed to the place in numbers. In 1852 the Government had offered William Bent twelve thousand dollars for the fort, but Bent had demanded sixteen thousand, and when his figure was not accepted he had moved out and blown up the place.

What was left served as an abode for the handlers who tended the stage horses. Still, the Rio Kid and his trail partners had found satisfactory accommodations.

"I reckon we might as well mosey on to Santa Fe," said the Rio Kid as they neared Bent's Fort with their day's bag. "Reckon we've seen all the excitement in these parts, Major."

"Yuh're right." North nodded. He coughed, his bony frame shaken by the spasm. But he took it as a matter of course. Danger, sickness, not even death could overawe Frank North.

■ ■ ■ ■

Celestino Mireles was pleased at the decision to head for New Mexico. He had relatives there, as he did along the Border from the Gulf coast up through San Antonio and into California. Though he was homeless, through choice, his family was large, and always welcomed him.

The sun gilded the mountain peaks and slanted across the river, turning Bent's Fort golden. The walls of the Fort had caved in, but corrals and sheds had been thrown up, and the place was still picturesque.

It was still light when the Rio Kid and his companions reached the station. A Concord stage stood in front. The dusty, weary teams had been unhitched, and the few passengers — drummers and two ladies — were inside consuming what passed for supper. Meals were notoriously poor at such spots, so much so that the Rio Kid and his friends did their own cooking.

A bearded, dirty man, with frowsy brown hair, and wearing stained pants and shirt, and old cowboots, shifted his tobacco cud as they rode up. He was rubbing down a sweated horse which had harness galls on its shoulders.

He was Jack Hobbs, the station keeper. He was married to an Indian woman. The squaw served all those around the station. A couple of dark-skinned boys, sons of Hobbs and the squaw, came to unload the meat.

"Say, Rio Kid!" called Hobbs. "An hombre come in this afternoon askin' for yuh. He's sleepin' over there by the shed. Shore is a mess."

Bob Pryor dropped Saber's rein and hurried around the crude shelter. He stared at the battered figure lying on his back. He was a big man who wore leather trousers, moccasins, and a belt. His bronzed torso was naked and criss-crossed by thorn scratches and red welts from whipping branches. His face was smeared and his dark hair matted with sweat, caked with mud, and thick with stickers. It took the Rio Kid several minutes to identify Steelhide Cass.

He stooped and shook Cass awake. As the Rio Kid knew, Steelhide usually slept on a hair trigger, but he was utterly exhausted now, and it was a minute before he was awake enough to talk.

"Rio Kid!" he shouted then. "Shore glad I caught yuh here! Thought I might have to run all the way to Santa Fe."

"What's wrong?" demanded the Rio Kid.

147

"Daggett! He turned the train to the mine, but it ain't gold. It's a rich copper lode, and it's his. He's enlisted Bull Fanning and his band, disarmed the folks, and forced 'em to work the mine. Galusha Shannon ordered me to find you. I shore hope we can get back before it's too late!"

Chapter XIV

BOLD PLAY

Pryor listened with a sober face to Steelhide's story. He felt his anger mounting, against Webb Daggett, and against the rascals enlisted by the man. It was no part of the Rio Kid's character for him to enjoy smug satisfaction because the wagon train people had made an error when they had turned away from him. He felt only sympathy for them as he quickly gauged the situation.

"Sounds bad, Cass," he said. "Daggett is apt to lash out and start killin' to cover himself on account of yore escape."

"That's what I kept tellin' myself," declared Steelhide grimly. "I was run 'way off course into the mountains but managed to shake 'em off and reach here. We got to move fast and even then it may be all over by now. Yuh must count on facin' eighty gunslingers, what with Fanning's bunch and men Daggett has won over, like Watts and

Lynch."

The Rio Kid hunted in his quick mind for allies. Sante Fe was a long run from here, and there were no fighters at Bent's; just a handful of men of Hobbs' caliber.

"Let's have a quick bite, Steelhide," suggested the Rio Kid. "I'll talk to North and see what he says. One thing's certain — if we hope to save Shannon and the rest we can't waste any time gettin' back to Daggettville."

Steelhide Cass limped after him around the shed. The stage driver, an elegant, mustached Frontier personage, was saying to Hobbs, in a loud voice: "I tell yuh that Holliday will throw us all out of work before long, with his railroad! His graders are 'way into Kansas right now. Back in Missouri they're givin' ten to one that Holliday can't reach the Colorado line by March, which he has to do if he's to win the Government grant.

"But I talked with the Colonel just two nights ago! He had a passel of surveyors, engineers and bridge builders, shortcuttin' through, savvy? Tracklayin' is fast over the prairie, and Holliday aims to have everything ready when they come with the rails. I'd lay ten to one Holliday gets that grant."

The Rio Kid paused beside the driver.

"Where did yuh meet up with Holliday?" he asked.

"Yuh savvy the big rapids at the Bend?" said the stage driver. "He was camped by a ravine they got to bridge, but I understood they were near through and would head this direction."

"How many with him?"

"Oh, thirty to forty. And don't let anybody tell yuh them railroadeers ain't tough hombres!"

Driven as he was with the knowledge that haste was imperative, still the Rio Kid yet knew he must not rush in without plans that would have at least a chance of success. Mireles was carving antelope steaks and North started a wood fire as the Rio Kid led Steelhide Cass aside and explained the situation. North immediately came to the same grave conclusion as had Bob Pryor.

"If we make it I'll be s'prised, Rio Kid."

Later, as they consumed a strengthening meal, they all talked the situation over.

"We'll hustle to Daggettville, the four of us, and smash through after dark," said the Rio Kid. "Mebbe we can arm some of our friends there, and hold on till help comes. We can't waste time, or take chances of bein' too late."

"And where can we find such help?"

inquired North. "There's none hereabouts we could count on."

"I got an idea," went on the Rio Kid. "Hobbs has a boy of around fifteen, as good a rider as I ever saw. He's a pard of mine as yuh savvy, since we stopped here, and he'll carry a message for me to a place I picked out for it to go."

After they had drunk coffee, and packed rations, they collected what arms they could. The lad had already ridden east from the stage station with the Rio Kid's letter. They bought what spare weapons and ammunition Hobbs would sell, dumped these in a bag and set out on the Santa Fe Trail under the stars, back toward the Daggettville turnoff. With his three companions the Rio Kid was gambling his life in the hope he might save the luckless victims of Daggett's savagery.

They made a quick trip to Daggettsville where, outside the town, they shot a way through the ring of sentries, and outdistanced them in a race for the settlement.

The Rio Kid with Frank North at his heels hurried across the porch of Daggett's saloon and paused in the wide front doorway. Mireles held three lathered horses in the shadows and the young Mexican marksman could help protect his friends' rear as they boldly pushed into the enemy den.

Andrew Cass with the bag of guns and bullets had dropped off and was hastily rousing and arming as many of the men of the caravan as he could.

The Rio Kid, Colts loaded and ready, and a sawed-off shotgun over one arm, swept the big room with quick blue eyes. Full-house Watts in his dandy's clothing was at the gaming table. Nutcracker Lynch hung over the crude bar, sodden with red-eye as he boasted to a group of Fanning outlaws and drover cronies. The odors of stale food, tobacco smoke and spilled whisky filled the place.

"Hey, there's Clay Allison of Las Animas," murmured North, from his position at Pryor's right hand. "Must be outsiders have already heard of the new town and some have come to look it over."

That was understandable to the Rio Kid, where this Clay Allison was concerned. The Rio Kid, like most others in that country, knew much of Clay Allison, knew he was usually on the hunt for excitement, wherever it might be found.

Allison was a strikingly handsome young man who like to hurrah the Kansas cow-camps. It was said that Clay would shoot a man just to see him kick, and was willing to fight a Northerner any time.

Now Allison was engrossed in the cards dealt by Fullhouse Watts, and when the gambler, seeing the Rio Kid, uttered a screech of alarm, nearly upsetting the table as he dived under it, Clay Allison was annoyed.

"What's goin' on?" he shouted angrily. He turned hot brown eyes on the Rio Kid.

His black hair waved about a poetic brow, his bold face was set off by a close-cropped black mustache and goatee. Allison was six feet tall but was handicapped by a club foot. Anyone who so much as dared look at it, however, would have to eat lead. Tonight he wore new clothing — a checked shirt and tight-fitting gray trousers.

But the Rio Kid had his hands too full to give much attention to Clay Allison. Pryor discounted Fullhouse Watts, who feared him so, and he let Nutcracker Lynch go for the moment, since the ox driver was drunk as a lord. The Rio Kid's eyes were on a side door which had been flung open to disclose Webb Daggett, who had caught the warning called by Fullhouse. The sentinels, too, following up the invading quartet, were closing it on the gulch, firing and whooping it up as they came.

"That's the Rio Kid!" howled Daggett. "Kill him!" He threw up the Navy revolver he gripped.

The Rio Kid, in a fighting crouch with his booted feet spread, wanted Daggett most of all. But in front of Daggett towered a huge figure in black leather. The man nearly touched the ceiling with the top of his shiningly bald, square head. The massive Bull Fanning. The outlaw chief whipped his silver-inlaid Colts from their holsters.

The Rio Kid made his choice. His shotgun roared, one barrel, then the second. He hoped to hit two birds at once as the buck shrieked through the hot air, spreading as it flew. Bull Fanning caught the heavy charges through the body. He was ripped wide open and his pistols cracked harmlessly, not yet high enough to pin North or the Rio Kid.

Daggett, if hit, still had the strength to fall back and slam the door.

Major North's revolver roared as a slug kicked up dirt from the packed-clay floor. Nutcracker Lynch, pulling himself together, was in action.

North's bullet slashed the ox driver, tore his right shoulder, and threw him around. Lynch went down on one knee, biting at his lip in pain. The mighty Bull Fanning, his luck run out at last, was shuddering in death as he lay on his face before Daggett's quarters.

The Rio Kid hurled the shotgun away and pulled a Colt.

"Reach for the rafters!" he ordered, sweeping the saloon.

North let go again. Nutcracker Lynch had refused to surrender and the Major's bullet drove into Lynch's heart. Seeing that, others in the room stunned by the force displayed by the Rio Kid and Frank North, raised their hands.

Clay Allison rose to his feet, scowling. He could draw and fire with lightning speed, but he made no move toward his guns.

"Yuh've busted up my game!" he complained.

"Keep out of this, Clay," warned the Rio Kid. "This ain't yore fight. Take my advice. Jump on yore warhoss and ride."

The egotistical Allison was furious. But he knew the Rio Kid and Major North, and quickly made his decision. He would not raise his hands but swung and strode to the bar, stepping over the body of Nutcracker Lynch without even a glance at the dead drover. He poured himself a cupful of whisky and downed it, his back to the Rio Kid.

A shot outside and a call from Mireles sent the Rio Kid streaking to the front door while North held the men in the saloon with steady gun.

"Daggett!" yelled Celestino. "He ees run around back. He limp, he have peestol. Look out for ze windows."

There was action, too, below the saloon. Steelhide Cass was frantically hailing the Rio Kid. In the lull following the swift scrap in the bar, Pryor could hear Cass' great voice over the approaching hubbub raised by Fanning's main bunch.

"They're comin', Rio Kid! This way — this way. Hustle, before it's too late."

A bullet spat into the wooden wall not a foot from North. The Rio Kid saw the flash at the back window. It might be Daggett or one of the chief's men who had not been trapped inside. Daggett was ordering help, and there were plenty of his aides driving in. The surprise was over and Daggett was rallying his forces.

"Outside, Major!" the Rio Kid said, and North jumped back.

The three leaped on their horses and pelted toward the cabins. Cass was waiting for them.

"I got 'em all up above, behind Shannon's and another camp," Cass informed.

"There's a thin line tryin' to hold back Fanning's gunhands."

"Is Shannon alive?" asked Pryor.

"Yeah, but he's hurt some. Daggett has been workin' on him and on Gregg and Jake Cochran."

In the darkness the Rio Kid pulled his fighters behind little shacks and boulders over the trail. Masses of armed riders surged past, shooting at shadows as Webb Daggett egged them on. Daggett was taking over and quickly set his followers to hold in Bob Pryor and the rest of the insurgents. A chunk of buckshot had slashed Daggett, but had not stopped him.

For the moment the Rio Kid was content to lie in cover and just hold Daggett off. He needed to regain his breath and estimate what strength he had. He had brought in all the pistols and carbines he could obtain, but the ammunition was limited.

He was sure that dawn would bring a showdown.

CHAPTER XV

BY THE GUN

Roaring of the mountain torrent echoed from the stone walls of Daggettville Gulch. The whitish-gray mists rising from the damp grasses and earth were blowing away in the morning light and gradually objects took on form for the tense men held down by Daggett's gunslingers.

Before dawn the Rio Kid had relayed orders to the women and children and those who could not participate in the battle for them to barricade themselves inside the thick log walls of their cabins and wait until the outcome was decided.

Galusha Shannon was lying in his bunk, with Sari at his side. Shannon was weak, for Daggett had maltreated the elderly man after Steelhide Cass had escaped. Finally, Daggett had forced Shannon to sign over credits with which to exploit the great copper deposits. Silas Gregg, too, and others who had money in Eastern banks had suffered.

Back of the Shannon home crouched the Rio Kid, Steelhide Cass and Mireles. Major North held Gregg's cabin with Quincy Warren, who thirsted for vengeance against the men who had killed his son. In other strategic spots the McCoys, Al Boyd and George Oaks, and other marksmen of the wagon train waited. But they were poorly armed and any concerted charge would quickly exhaust what ammunition the Rio Kid had been able to run in on the hurried trip from Bent's.

The Rio Kid peered around the north end of the cabin. A rifle slug sent from a saloon window cut a chunk from the pine log which sheltered him and rapped into the rocks of the cliff. He tried the south, and was again fired on by Daggett's crew. The gunhands of the deceased Bull Fanning, and traitors among the wagon train group who had gone over to Daggett, made up a formidable aggregation.

"I don't like that bluff behind us, Steelhide," remarked the Rio Kid, glancing over his shoulder at the towering cliff. Brush fringed the lip far overhead.

"They can work around if they think of it," agreed Cass. "I climbed up that big split the night I got away from here, Rio Kid."

"Send word along that if they open on us from above the boys are to take to the cabins," ordered Pryor. "It's the only way."

His command was passed from one group to another. The light was increasing and Webb Daggett, perhaps sensing that time was important, suddenly began his attack.

From the saloon, from spots of cover angling in at the besieged, heavy gunfire broke out. Daggett's followers were dismounted, and were protected by thick walls or rising rocks.

"Keep down!" roared the Rio Kid, signaling his fighting men.

Lead spattered into the cliff or clipped the edges of the cabin logs. Powder smoke rose slowly in the gulch.

The Rio Kid was still worried about the rear. He kept looking up at the cliff. Suddenly smoke puffs spurted from the brush as the gulch rang with deafening explosions. A wagon train man named Hank Hons threw up his hands and pitched forward.

Major North whirled as lead whistled within an inch of his ear. Instantly he, as well as Cass and the Rio Kid, covered the ragged lip of the cliff with bullets. Pryor's fighters began entering the cabins through rear windows and doors. Hons was carried in to his home and his bride hovered over him, seeking to ease his pain.

Slugs which came close sought the Rio Kid, but he was moving fast, and joined Steelhide Cass, Galusha and Sari in the Shannon home. There, square openings cut in the front and back walls served as windows, and the Rio Kid took a stand at the side of one of them, where he could command the slope from the trail.

The burst of guns echoed away and they heard Daggett's powerful voice in the lull.

"Go in and take 'em!"

Heavily armed outlaws leaped up, rushing the shacks at Daggett's command: Cursing lieutenants urged them on. They came thick and fast, stooped over as they charged. Many gripped sawed-off shotguns or heavy rifles.

The Rio Kid took a deep breath. "Now or never," he thought. To break such an attack, plenty of ammunition would be required — and they didn't have much!

"Let 'em have it, boys!" he bellowed.

Cass stood at the side of a window. Mireles had the slab door propped open a few inches so he could fire through the opening. They worked their carbines at full speed, picking off ambitious bandits, cutting them with tearing metal.

A hundred feet from the row of cabins the

hirelings faltered. Daggett was safe in the saloon, watching from a peep-hole. His enraged voice shrieked at his killers but the Rio Kid's people were putting all they had into the struggle.

A Daggett man turned and ran back, throwing himself behind his rock. Then three more quit. The rout became general as Fanning's toughs refused to face death by frontal assault. Dust and wisps of smoke hung over the ravine, but the mountain torrent gushed blindly on as men fought and died.

"We ain't got many loads left," muttered the Rio Kid, wiping the sweat from his eyes, and handling his hot guns gingerly.

"Another rush and we're through," growled Steelhide Cass.

Sari Shannon touched his arm, smiling up at him. From his bed, Galusha Shannon said:

"It's best to die fightin', boys. I'll go along with you."

From the saloon Daggett was urging his aides to try again, but the outlaws had not enjoyed the taste of what had already been given them. The sun rose higher, slanting into the gulch, heating the shacks as its rays beat on the roofs. Its heat would soon bring thirst, but water was not a problem. Pans and jars had been filled in all the cabins — a necessary precaution, for though the cool little river was not far off, death would meet anyone venturing near it.

The tension held. The besieged people glimpsed Webb Daggett now and then, but he was too far off to be a target. Big boulders were rolled off the cliff, but only one building was damaged and no one in it was hurt.

The afternoon dragged along, the Rio Kid and his men holding firm. He had no other intention in mind, since he, North, Cass and Mireles had purposely cut off any possible escape for themselves by turning loose their horses. Somewhere on the plain Saber and the other mounts ran free, waiting.

"Will he come?" the Rio Kid kept thinking. Had his message gone through?

The sun was dropping on the west of the ravine when the Rio Kid, peering from the window corner, heard a shrill whistle, and guessed what it meant. Daggett must have argued the bandits into another attempt to storm the shacks.

Again the defenders saw ferocious figures leap from cover and start at them. But this time they did not have the means by which to slash the running line. Windows and cracks were filled with driving lead which held down the hidden sharpshooters.

Steelhide Cass let go his last bullet and turned to Sari, taking her in his arms. The Rio Kid had a few slugs left, but he knew almost all the ammunition must now be gone, since there was only a scattering volley from the cabins.

He bobbed up to send a shot into a big fellow who was charging straight at Shannon's camp. Then the Rio Kid gave a loud shout of triumph at what he saw. For, entering the southern end of the gulch, came a band of riders armed to the teeth. There were between thirty and forty, stalwart men in corduroys or leather, bearded, and with felt hats strapped on firmly.

In a single glance the Rio Kid recognized Cyrus Holliday, the Santa Fe railroad man, Tom Peters, his builder, and Captain Ellingwood, head surveyor for the line. The others were young engineers and workers in Holliday's employ. Fearless young Jackie Hobbs, the slim half-breed who had carried Pryor's plea for aid to Holliday, had come along. He had brought along his light carbine with which he was expert. He rode his gray mustang with lithe grace.

"This way, Santa Fe!" roared the Rio Kid.

Holliday heard him. His usually pleasant

face was stern now. The Rio Kid saw Holliday's side whiskers waggle as the man turned and snapped commands.

Daggett's crew immediately realized the threat to them, and that the oncoming riders could quickly turn the tide. For the gunslingers were in the open, easy targets.

Holliday's men lined out rapidly, and threw up carbines, shotguns and Colts.

"Throw down your weapons!" shouted Holliday, his voice ringing through the gulch.

The hired gunslingers swerved off toward the protection of the saloon. They fully realized at what a disadvantage they had been caught, dismounted as they were, and with their horses to the south, out of easy range. A few of them sent wild slugs at the railroaders but the bursts from Holliday's forces checked concerted resistance. The riders quickly came up with the bandits before they could take cover. Most of the outlaws threw down their guns in surrender.

The Rio Kid rushed from the Shannon cabin, calling to Holliday. Jackie Hobbs whooped at him, Saber, the Rio Kid's mouse-colored dun, trained warhorse, had followed the arriving riders into the ravine road. The mount came trotting up as the

Rio Kid whistled.

As he seized the bridle and vaulted into leather, the Rio Kid saw Webb Daggett, with Fullhouse Watts at his heels, run out of the saloon and start up the narrowing cut. On the dun, Bob Pryor galloped after his arch-enemy.

Watts saw him first and shrieked to Daggett, whose long legs had taken him out ahead.

"Turn yore face to the bank and keep yore hands clasped over yore head, Watts!" shouted the Rio Kid, his Colt up and the spur back under his thumb.

The gambler was gasping for wind. He fell to his knees, but did not attempt to fight, putting his hands up as ordered.

Daggett was not far ahead as the Rio Kid streaked past Fullhouse Watts. Daggett had a Navy pistol in one hand and glanced back, his flecked eyes glinting, his face twitching. His nose, which looked so like a wedge of pale cheese, offered a target.

Daggett swore as he fired, the bullet driving past the Rio Kid's left shoulder. The dun swerved and the Rio Kid's quick shot missed. But he was almost upon Daggett, who whirled, and crouched for the kill.

The two revolvers seemed to crackle together. But it was Daggett whose arm dropped and who teetered, then fell over on his side, his nose smashed by the Rio Kid's lead, and a bullet in his evil brain.

The Rio Kid, with Frank North and Celestino at either side of him, led the caravan into Santa Fe.

They had picked up the horses and oxen from the plateau, loaded the wagons, and returned to the Trail. Passing Bent's Fort, and toiling through the rocks of Raton Pass and then along the Purgatoire, they had slowly skirted the foothills to Las Vegas. The Rio Kid had finally led them to their goal, the magic Santa Fe.

The old town lay at the foot of the Sangre de Cristo range. Low adobe huts and unpaved streets spread before their eyes as they topped the last rise and glimpsed the town. It was a new world, filled with Latin gaiety, with women in silks and satins and embroidered shawls, short skirts and low-necked chemises, with men in velvet and steeple sombreros.

It was another civilization, but glamorous to those who had been so long on the Trail. The towers of the cathedral rose over the flat rocks, and the warm scent of flowers filled the air.

The next day, when they had rested, the

Rio Kid spoke to his friends of the wagon train.

"From now on it's up to you folks what yuh do," he said gravely. "Galusha Shannon, Silas Gregg and Jake Cochran are willin' to finance that copper mine and take yuh all in on shares. It will make yuh well-to-do if yuh're willin' to work hard and get the metal out. Yuh can buy tools and provisions here and return to the gulch. Steelhide Cass says he'll boss operations. Mebbe yuh all savvy that he's marryin' Sari, and they aim to settle in Santa Fe."

Cheers rose for the Rio Kid and for Sari and Cass.

"You must share in the mine, Rio Kid," Galusha Shannon said.

But the captain of the wagon train shook his head.

"I'm no miner, folks. Like I promised back in Missouri, I've brought yuh through and that suits me fine. The Major's goin' to stick here a while and get over his sickness. Mireles and I are ridin' in the mornin'."

The wilderness called the Rio Kid and his Mexican *compadre.* Next day they hit the trail out of Santa Fe, turning to wave farewell to their charges. Danger they knew, lay ahead, as always but the Rio Kid, on the dun, headed toward it.

We hope you have enjoyed this Large Print book. Other Thorndike, Wheeler, and Chivers Press Large Print books are available at your library or directly from the publishers.

For information about current and upcoming titles, please call or write, without obligation, to:

Publisher
Thorndike Press
295 Kennedy Memorial Drive
Waterville, ME 04901
Tel. (800) 223-1244

or visit our Web site at:

http://gale.cengage.com/thorndike

OR

Chivers Large Print
published by BBC Audiobooks Ltd
St James House, The Square
Lower Bristol Road
Bath BA2 3SB
England
Tel. +44(0) 800 136919
email: bbcaudiobooks@bbc.co.uk
www.bbcaudiobooks.co.uk

All our Large Print titles are designed for easy reading, and all our books are made to last.